DEAR VALENTINE

Sharon couldn't help liking brave, kind Valentine, even though she had foolishly given her heart to Tony Martindale, his unworthy nephew. Her involvement with the Martindales began with an unexpected telephone call from a distraught young woman who called herself Shari. Inviting her near-namesake round for coffee, Sharon hoped she might be able to help in some way. But the impulse triggered off a macabre sequence of events.

Books by Anne Saunders
in the Linford Romance Library:

BEWARE THIS STRANGER

ANNE SAUNDERS

DEAR VALENTINE

Complete and Unabridged

LINFORD
Leicester

First published in Great Britain

First Linford Edition
published 1996

British Library CIP Data

Saunders, Anne
    Dear Valentine.—Large print ed.—
Linford romance library
1. English fiction—20th century
I. Title
823.9'14 [F]

ISBN 0–7089–7923–8

Published by
F. A. Thorpe (Publishing) Ltd.
Anstey, Leicestershire

Set by Words & Graphics Ltd.
Anstey, Leicestershire
Printed and bound in Great Britain by
T. J. Press (Padstow) Ltd., Padstow, Cornwall

This book is printed on acid-free paper

1

AS Sharon opened the outer door her lungs pulled in a deep, knifing breath and the sharp air bit her lips and froze her ears and the vulnerable bit of leg between hemline and boot. An early dusk, a lowering sky packed solid with the promise of more snow to come, was a further hazard to the motorists skidding helplessly on patches of black ice.

She was glad to be a pavement prowler as she slithered over the hard, frozen knobs of ice, to capsize crazily round each corner as she met the full blast of a rushing wind that grabbed greedily at the flapping edge of her coat and the feather valiantly aloft in her hat. Only an imbecile, or someone terribly hard up for the money, would be out on such a vile day when they could be home, eating mountains of hot, buttery toast, enfolded in the warmth of an open-hearth fire. Except that her bed-sit didn't boast an open hearth, only an inadequate popping gas fire which ate coins faster than she could produce them.

Perhaps she'd been stupid to opt for this life of loneliness when she could have been enjoying sunshine and companionship with Aunt Lucy and Cousin Simon in Australia. If only she'd had more time to decide. Aunt Lucy had thrust the idea at her at the very last moment, claiming to have saved it up as a special surprise. Pride had made her refuse, because it sounded too much like a conscience-stricken afterthought. So she had politely thanked her aunt for providing her with a home for the past ten years, since the death of her parents, and had tried to put behind her the unworthy thought that she had out-served her usefulness. Simon, at fourteen, was a big boy and no longer needed an on the spot, unpaid nursemaid.

Anyway, it was probably distance and separation that was gilding memory, painting a picture of eternal sunshine. Eternal anything must be boring after a while and, truthfully, she had never really got on with Aunt Lucy.

The towering supermarkets of an alien town slipped away and she gained the library cum museum. Perhaps she shouldn't have moved away from Timbrewick, but with Aunt Lucy and Simon gone, there had been no point in staying and, anyway, her job had folded up when old Mr. Carter died and in a village of that size the prospects of finding another were practically non-existent.

The road struck a slanting course. She applied her shoulder with all the strength she possessed to combat the increased velocity of the wind and first saw her assignment, Bonbon House, as an indistinct blur through wind-tear-whipped eyes. It was enough to see it did not live up to its delicious name. Four square and functional, Georgian, ugly, with a touch of Gothic in the shape of the high, pointed door, yet totally lacking the soaring grace and subtle delicacy of that period. Yet nothing had ever beckoned as welcoming as, limp of feather and limb, her numb fingers closed round the embellished brass knob.

Inside was an elegance undreamt of. A reception area with long cream couches, acres of glass-topped counter and a circulating warmth that drove hot pins under her finger-nails and enhanced the agony of her chilblain-prone little toe.

"You're new, aren't you?" enquired the receptionist. "I don't remember seeing you before."

"I haven't been with the agency long," admitted Sharon, realising she had been summed up and found wanting. She had been warned that this particular assignment might mean overtime. That's why she had been chosen, because she wasn't committed to rush home to anybody and not because of her outstanding efficiency, although she had been told that Martindale's used the agency quite often and was a valuable account. They were makers of confectionery, boiled sweets, liquorice comfits, that sort of thing.

The head of the firm, Valentine Martindale, was convalescing after a heart operation. His nephew, Tony Martindale, was deputising for him during his absence. One of the girls in the office had described him as a 'sweet man'.

"Miss Sharon Swift from the Helen Graham Typewriting Agency," the receptionist announced into a sherbert-pink telephone. Then Sharon was being led down a corridor and shunted into an office with three tender, toffee-cream walls and one of frosted glass. It was empty, but someone was in the office beyond. The striking silhouette of a man was etched on the glass and she could hear a gentle grumble of voices. One silhouette, yet voices? Obviously someone of a slighter build stood in front of the shadowy giant.

The plaintive cheeping of a hungry sparrow sent her eyes hopping towards the window. She saw an overcrowding of roof tops in mud-sludge colours, set at various angles. When she looked back it was to see two distinct silhouettes. The slighter one was moving towards the connecting door, opening it.

"Sorry to keep you waiting." It was a token apology because the eyes, a deep and compelling blue, almost purple, did not hold regret. Sharon judged they had viewed the world stoically, inquisitively, indifferently, depending on the mood of the moment, for close on thirty years. How many of them, she wondered, had it taken to acquire that special confidence, that enviable polish, and in eight years' time, when she was thirty, would she have achieved it?

It was doubtful. For one thing she didn't have a Botticelli underlip, or grape-dark hair piled in loose Grecian curls. One of the curls had come adrift and was flopping like a floating corkscrew against the girl's white throat. Who was she? Super secretary? Very personal assistant? On the breath of that thought a hand went up to push back the curl with a fussy, telling movement which explained the one silhouette on the frosted glass. Amiable relations all round, thought Sharon. And giggled.

It wasn't hard to guess the identity of the man. She had been forewarned of Tony Martindale's charm and susceptibility. Although he hadn't been with the firm all that long, apparently he had stepped into the breach when his uncle became ill, he had intimate knowledge of the sweet-making industry and was — how had her informant worded it? — recently back from the Continent a powerful export order heavier, having toted his samples with success and enterprise. End of confidence because she had been told to enterprise herself round to Bonbon House, with a snappy, but unfounded surely? warning to *Watch it*.

She considered that most unjust. Just because she had green eyes and in some ways resembled a rascally Robin Hood, it didn't automatically follow she went round stealing from the rich. Rich in companionship that is. That made her want to giggle again. This time she dealt with the undesirable impulse more severely, so that only a soupçon of humour stirred her eyes. Anyway, even if she wanted to she couldn't rob this lovely creature of anything. Not with that face as protection.

The girl introduced herself simply as: "Moira." She showed her where to hang her hat and coat and the whereabouts of the electric power point for the inevitable cup of coffee. Then, without so much as a lift of an apologetic eyebrow, loaded her with a formidable amount of work. To catch the evening post.

"And for my next miracle," said Sharon, attacking a new ream of typing paper.

"Just do your best," she drawled, and

8

the smile which limped to her mouth was crippled with indifference. Amiable up to a point, amended Sharon, and her nose wrinkled because she hadn't much time for the sort of female who only staged the charm for a masculine audience.

But what charm. She perceived it again shortly before six o'clock when a broad hand, with capable spatula shaped tips, rested on the connecting door. The smile threw away its crutches and ran in effusive welcome to meet the glint in the sweet man's treacle-brown, liquorice dark eyes. They had to look up quite a bit because he was tall, a rangy six foot plus, and Sharon thought he had been miscast as a sweet man because he had the length and breadth, and the physical vivacity of a lumberjack; darkly grained hair, like polished oak, square purposeful jaw, and teeth so white and even they looked as if they'd never bitten into a soft and sugary sweetmeat.

"How's it going, Moira?" he asked.

"Not too bad," she understated.

"Good, good." He attached himself to the desk Sharon occupied, hanging one leg over the corner in a relaxed, half-sitting position. He borrowed the receptionist's dialogue.

"Hello. You're new, aren't you?"

"Yes. I only started with the agency a few weeks ago."

"Don't apologise," he said perceptively. "I'm sure you are very efficient." Little did he know what a bungler she was, thought Sharon wryly. Yet she wasn't always to blame. She didn't purposely hatch the improbable situations she found herself in. Take yesterday. Could she have known that the lock on the stock-room door was going to jam at minutes to home time, and that if a colleague hadn't happened by, a lucky chance if ever there was one, she would have had to resort to a trap-door and an unspeakably dirty loft as a means of exit? A memory she happily relinquished in time to hear him say:

"They wouldn't send anyone who couldn't cope. But it's an overtime job and they usually choose — What I mean is, a pretty thing like you must have someone to rush home to."

Oh! he was nice. Her eyes stretched up to tell him so, her mouth framed a: "No, no one."

"No one?" The inflection of surprise in his voice hoisted her spirits and her delight soared disproportionately, A temperamental cough, a timely reminder that the bit actress is never allowed to steal the scene, returned things to their proper perspective. With the ease of experience, Moira came and stood next to Tony. Her nose turned into his neck.

"Darling, you're prying."

"I'm not. I'm showing a kindly interest."

"All right. All right. Now let's go."

"In a minute." He wasn't going to be rushed. With slow deliberation he turned back to Sharon and said: "You don't mind being left on your own?"

"Really, Tony," said Moira with an exasperated click of her tongue.

"She won't be entirely on her own. The cleaning woman will be somewhere on the premises."

"I shall be all right," assured Sharon.

★ ★ ★

The switchboard was closed down for the night. The offices on either side were silent and empty and, although she wouldn't have admitted it to anyone, the cleaning woman's off-key rendering of a current pop hit was a welcome assault to her ears. There was comfort in the thought that she was not entirely alone.

The telephone, which for the last hour had sat silent and placid at her elbow, suddenly rang. The noise was so unexpected and imperious that she typed a wrong letter. The telephonist's last duty of the day was to plug the line through to this office, not strictly speaking to receive in-coming calls, at this time of day there weren't expected to be any, but so that Tony, who was usually the last to leave, could make a call if he so wished.

Sharon stared at the ringing instrument for an uncertain moment, then lifted the receiver.

"Martindale's," she announced; for want of something better to say, added: "May I help you, please?" That sounded less stark and, she thought, struck a friendlier note.

"That's not Moira." It wasn't a question, but a statement. As if the caller was attuned to Moira's telephone voice.

"No, it's not," confirmed Sharon. A curious wood-pecking noise was coming down the line. She couldn't identify it.

"Then who is it?"

"Sharon Swift," obliged Sharon. "But you won't know me. I'm temporary. There's no one here but me," she added unhelpfully, forgetting the cleaning woman. She was still puzzling over the wood-pecking noise. It was consistent with a beak against bark, or a woman's long finger nails nervously tapping a telephone mouth piece. Come to think of it, the voice carried a matching tenseness.

"Oh dear," it said, pitching low in desperation. "I thought I might just catch Tony. I must speak to him. I must . . . " She paused to collect herself. When she spoke again her voice was less fraught, disciplined to sound natural.

"I came to town to arrange a dental appointment for my small daughter. She . . . she bit into something hard and snapped off a tiny piece of tooth. It should be attended to." Sharon thought she was referring to the tooth, until she said: "I don't know what to do. It's such an incredible thing to happen. I must contact Tony. He'll tell me what I must do."

"I'm sorry," said Sharon inadequately. She knew what it was to be alone, to have a problem locked inside and have nobody there to listen. And advise.

"Look, I might not be able to help, I might not be equipped to, but sometimes it helps just to talk. Begin by telling me your name." To identify the caller was a logical first step.

"Shari Marshall."

"Shari," repeated Sharon, gaining thinking time. "It's very much like my name, only prettier. Where are you?"

"At the station."

"Bus or railway?"

"Railway. I'm . . . I'm waiting for a train. I was going to go back without telling and then I thought — Look, I'm sorry, you must have things to do. If you don't know where Tony is I'll — "

"Don't ring off," said Sharon, realising how tenuous a telephone connection is. "I've just had a thought. Why not catch a later train? Why not grab a taxi and come round here?"

"What for?" There was a feminine inconsequence of suspicion and yearning in her tone.

15

"To talk or not to talk," said Sharon, striving to sound casual and indifferent. "I'm not doing anything tonight. I shall be glad of your company." Her sincerity rang true.

There was a pause, a quick intake of breath, a relaxing, then: "I'll take you up on that. I'll try Tony's flat first. If he's not in, I'll be with you in fifteen minutes. Get the coffee cracking."

"Will do," said Sharon, feeling extremely pleased with herself. "It's started snowing again. So take care."

She finished typing the last letter, signed it, as Moira had told her to, and folded it into its envelope. She had grown used to the warmth that had at first overpowered her, and her fingers felt cold and stiff. Outside it was snowing goose feathers. She plugged in the electric kettle. Yes, coffee would be welcome — and wondered about Shari and what she was to Tony. She spooned instant coffee into cups with flat bottoms, rather like mugs only prettier than mugs, beautifully fragile and patterned with Autumn leaves.

The water in the kettle boiled. The cleaning woman popped her head round the door to say she was off and for Sharon to drop the latch when she left. The snow swirled down, covering the sludge coloured roofs, transforming, obliterating the view.

Three quarters of an hour passed and Shari still hadn't shown up. So reluctantly, because the girl's — woman's? — nervousness and rock-bottom desperation had got under her skin, she thought she'd better call it a day. It's hard to tell a person's age by their face, impossible from a snatched phrase or two over the telephone. Sharon could only hope Shari wasn't a very young girl and was old enough to reason things out for herself. She drew comfort from the remembered richness of the tone, which hinted at maturity.

She washed the two cups, meticulously put the coffee and everything back in its proper place. Then, as instructed,

17

dropped the latch and walked out into a blizzard of diamonds which stung her cheeks, adhered to her eyelashes and swarmed into her eyes.

She lowered her head and crunched her way slowly home. The cold penetrated her sheepskin coat and fleecy lined mittens, and she vowed that once she reached her room she wouldn't venture out again. Not for any consideration. Drab as it was, it suddenly became very desirable.

As she opened the door of the gaunt, ugly house, the peevish wind gave her a push from behind, hurling her in and liberally icing the entrance hall with a powdering of sugar-fine snowflakes.

"I hope you wiped your feet." Her landlady stood in her usual position by the door. Sharon suspected she stationed herself there permanently, waiting to catch her out in some slip.

"Yes, Mrs. Lamb," she said agreeably enough, thinking she had never seen anyone who looked less like a lamb. Her teeth were clenched and chattering as she streaked up the stairs, and her fingers were almost too frozen to fit the key in the lock.

She switched on the light, shunted herself out of her boots and thankfully cast off the hampering chilly wetness of her coat. Her poor little hat, with its forlorn feather, she twirled towards the peg; it missed, but she didn't bother to retrieve it from the floor.

Her toes were snug in slippers, her hands curved round a hot drink; she was drifting into blissful warmth, when she began to think about Shari, the girl on the phone. It spoilt her content of the moment because she felt she ought to do something, but she didn't know what it was she ought to do. She didn't know why she should be plagued in this way. After all, she had done her best. She had nothing to reproach herself for, but still the feeling of unease persisted. Why, she didn't know. Goodness, it ought to be Tony fretting it out. After all it was his distraught friend. Girl-friend?

Ex-girl-friend? The possibilities were endless. If she was his ex-girl-friend, because they'd had a tiff or because he'd thrown her over for someone else, Moira, for instance — they'd seemed to be on more than chummy terms — shouldn't he be told she'd phoned and was upset?

Yet she didn't know Shari was going to do anything foolish. Then again, she didn't know she was going to adopt the sensible attitude, think: There's more men than Tony on the face of the earth. And go out and buy herself a new dress or whatever jilted females do to better their morale. Never having been on close enough terms to be jilted, she didn't know.

She did know the sweetened drink in her hand suddenly tasted as sour as the situation she found herself in. She didn't want to telephone Tony Martindale on so delicate a matter, and yet if she didn't, sleep wouldn't be forthcoming that night.

Out again, ploughing towards the

telephone kiosk at the corner of the street, head down, slipping, slithering, labouring to breathe because the rawness of the wind was like a knife in her lungs. Her fingers tingled painfully, but not her feet. They were so numb they might have been sawn off at the knees.

She found his number in the directory, not the Bonbon House number, but the one listed alongside his private address. Tony Martindale, 15 Engles Court. That, she knew, was in the better part of town. Some houses, but mostly flats.

Having plucked up both phone and courage, it was a relief to hear the dialling tone. The snow had wrought havoc, isolating towns, bringing down telephone wires. That the phone was actually working seemed little short of a miracle. She knew she was being ridiculous, making a lot out of nothing, but by then it was almost a compulsion to get through, to discharge this final duty and get Shari out of her hair.

"Tony Martindale," said a voice, sounding beautifully like the right voice. She fumbled to put her money in the slot and said:

"Hello. This is Sharon Swift, the girl from the typewriting agency."

"Tony Martindale here," repeated the voice; he confirmed he hadn't heard a word she'd said by saying: "If anybody's there, speak up. This line is atrocious."

"I'm speaking up," yelled Sharon. "Can you hear me now?"

"I can hear something," he acknowledged. "You sound to be a million miles away. What's your name?"

"Sharon Swift."

"Sorry, you're not coming through. Try again."

"Sharon — " The Swift part was drowned in a burst of interference, a deafening bang-crackle of noise, but miraculously he seemed to have heard something; his voice lost its former clarity and was coming to her in waves of loud and faint. She heard him say,

22

"Where are you speaking from — ?" Then nothing.

"The telephone box at the corner of Blacksmith Street," she shouted.

She caught the words, "Good," and "Wait." Then silence again. He'd cut the connection. Towards the end he'd seemed to be able to hear her, so presumably she was to wait until he came. After about five minutes she left the telephone kiosk to peer up and down the street. She was beginning to dither in her boots again; not from cold, but because it was, on reflection, a bit silly. She didn't think he'd thank her for getting him out on a wild goose chase. She tugged her scarf — she'd abandoned for ever her cute, ruined hat — more firmly about her head and pulled up her coat collar, cursing her weirdly colourful imagination.

Phantom white cars crawled down the street, a drunken, ghostly caravan of vehicles in a desert of whiteness. One car manoeuvred with less caution and squealed to a stop at the curb.

The door wrenched open and she was snatched up to a manly chest.

Perhaps the numbness that robbed her of feet had seeped into her brain depriving her of reason, because for a brief, wonderful moment she revelled in the bliss of being anchored in this masculine bear-hug, and delighted in the sensation of warmth as his emotion spilled over her like liquid joy. His hands pulled down her headscarf to ruffle her hair and his breath felt hot on her forehead as he choked out words.

"It's wonderful . . . a miracle . . . I can't believe it. They told me you were — " That was all he could manage. Something warm and wet fell on her forehead. "It's a miracle," he repeated. "Oh Shari,"

Shar-i. The termination burst in her brain, freeing it of inertia. Not Sharon. *Shari*. He thought —

Her mouth opened to correct his mistake, but perhaps her lack of response, her very stillness did it for her, or maybe he suddenly looked at her because he tore himself away, gasping:

"You're not Shari."

"I never said I was," said Sharon.

"But you did, on the telephone," he protested. "You said you were Shari. Oh, my God." Her visibility of him was limited, but she spied a crazed frenzied look in his eye that was frightening, and a pained, sad look that was inexplicable and in its own way more frightening still. He put his hands up, hiding his face, his vulnerability. When they drew away he was composed, with only a hint of the inner struggle and sadness.

"How could you do such a vicious, cruel thing?" he asked icily.

She looked up at him, perplexed. "I'm sorry, Mr. Martindale. I don't know what you mean."

"Don't you?" His face was far removed from her in a floating sea of snow, but she could imagine the bitter, disbelieving set of his mouth.

"No, honestly, I haven't the faintest

idea what you are talking about. You must believe me."

"Must I?" He was a robot man, a man in deep shock. "Why must I?"

"Because I don't honestly know what it's all about. Oh, I realise from your manner something has happened. Something has happened to — Shari?"

"Did you know Shari?"

"No, I only — " Spoke to her on the telephone, she was going to say when something, a premonition perhaps, stilled her tongue. "No, I didn't know her," she said, freezing at the tense. He'd said 'Did you know her?' Not 'Do you know her?'

"Your loss. Because now you never will." He sounded hard and uncaring and she might have believed him but for the memory of that tear scalding her forehead.

"She died just this evening."

2

NOW it was Sharon's turn to shake her head in disbelief. She wanted to shout 'No, it's not true.' Shari *couldn't* be dead. She'd spoken to her not much more than three hours ago. People don't just die, not unless they're very old and in the sunset of life. And then it's not death, hard and cold and final, a severing of breath and friendship and earthly contact with loved ones; but the soul's release from its poor worn-out body.

Perhaps Shari wasn't young. Perhaps she wasn't a girlfriend at all, but a relative, an aged relative who had served the apprenticeship of life and —

No, it wouldn't fit. Shari had a small daughter. On the telephone she'd said in her lovely rich *young* voice, 'I came to town to arrange a dental appointment for my small daughter.'

An aged relative wouldn't have a small daughter. What *was* Shari to Tony Martindale?

"My sister. She was my sister," he said in a dazed voice, just as if he had been sitting in on her thoughts. Or had she, in her agitation, perhaps voiced the question? "They'd only just informed me when you phoned. I thought they'd made a mistake, although identification was pretty conclusive. She had papers on her, including a letter with my name and address on it. That's why they contacted me. I didn't really reason it out. I don't suppose one does stop to reason a miracle. I thought — "

"How agonising for you," managed Sharon. "I don't know what to say. It's the similarity of our names that wrought the confusion. I never dreamt anything like this could happen. It's too dreadful for words. Sorry is so inadequate."

"I'd rather you didn't say anything. Just go."

It was natural that in his moment

of grief he couldn't bear the sight and sound of her. But:

"How — " Her throat was suddenly uncomfortably dry. "How did she die?"

"Hit and run. A car swerved off the road and ran into her. An eye witness said she came out of the station and was endeavouring to hail a taxi. Where was she going? That's what I keep asking myself. If she missed her train why didn't she phone me. That would have been the sensible thing to do."

Sharon could only stare at him like a mute. Enlarged emerald eyes blazed agonisingly in a face that was bleach-white. At the moment she hadn't the words to say 'She did telephone. She was coming to me. I invited her to her death. Because she had a problem and I was foolish enough, or pompous enough to think I could help. Whereas if I'd minded my own business and let her be, if I hadn't harangued her to set out, just when conditions were at their appalling worst, she would at this very moment be safe and well. Not — '

"Not your problem," he said nudging her arm. "Run along."

"In a minute. What . . . where are you going?"

"To the hospital. I have a rather unpleasant task to perform. A matter of identifying the body. I was ready to go, actually, when you phoned."

"Oh *no*!"

"Look," he said, "it's nice of you to be concerned, but it really is none of your business. Go home."

"I want to go to the hospital with you."

"Haven't you taken in a word I've said? I don't want you."

"Please. I won't talk. I won't even go in with you if you don't want me to. I'll sit in the car as quiet as a mouse. I don't want to intrude on your privacy; I just want to be alongside for a bit longer."

"No."

Only an idiot would persist after such a blunt refusal, an idiot, or someone eaten up with guilt.

"I promise not to get underfoot. Only *please*."

"All right," he capitulated ungraciously. Not because he welcomed her company, but because she was hanging on like a tenacious little dog he'd once owned; because he couldn't shake her off and moreover it was intensely cold and he was weary of this pointless bickering. And if that wasn't sufficient reason he wanted to get what had to be done, over and done with.

Afterwards, he steered her into an all night cafe. Self-service, down at heel. He hadn't noticed the pile of metal trays on the counter and heaved himself leadenly behind a conveniently placed table.

Sharon went to the counter, remembered, crossed the tiled floor to stand in front of him.

"I haven't enough money on me. I dashed out with only enough — " She bit her lip in agitation — "for the telephone. Could you?"

"What's that? Oh, of course." He

went to his pocket and scooped out a handful of change. Meticulously she selected the correct amount.

They sat sipping their tea, a gruesome twosome.

"Was it bad?"

"What do you think."

Silence.

"Is there anyone you should contact? Someone who ought to be informed?"

"No."

"Nobody? A husband, perhaps?"

"Shari has been, was," he corrected aggressively, "a widow for four years. Our parents died six years before that. There's nobody. Well, there's my uncle's wife, but she's enough to worry about at the moment with Uncle Val's illness. If you think I'm going to ring up at this time of night." He checked, looked at the wafer-thin gold watch strapping his wrist and amended that to, "morning, you're crazy."

"Sorry. I think I am a bit. It's an unhinging business. I thought whoever she lived with might worry when she doesn't report home."

"She lives — lived — with Uncle Valentine. It will have been assumed she has very sensibly booked in at a hotel, or is availing herself of my hospitality. Many's the time she's had my bed and I've lumped it on the sofa. Satisfied?"

"Yes."

"And now, do you think we might un-glue ourselves because I'm going home to bed. I take it you don't want to accompany me there as well?"

"No," said Sharon, crimson-cheeked.

★ ★ ★

"And where do you think you've been, Miss?"

The sight of her landlady, before she'd even pulled the door shut behind her, was almost too much for Sharon.

"Out."

However she managed to suppress the laugh, which wasn't a laugh but a

33

grotesque, hysterical bubbling of pent-up emotion, she would never know.

"Really!" gasped the outraged woman, her thin lips compressing to an even thinner line. "Do you know what time it is?"

"Late?" suggested Sharon defiantly.

"It's almost four a.m. I think you owe me an explanation."

Shari was dead. Her frustrations, her thoughts, her feelings had all died with her. And this upright, so-called Christian woman, who hadn't an ounce of Christian charity in her whole make-up, was looking at her as if she was a scarlet woman and demanding an explanation. Well, she could have one.

"I've been with a man," she said, indignation and seething outrage colouring her tone. "A man who has earned himself the reputation of eating little girls for supper."

"Are you crazy?"

"That's the second time that's been suggested tonight. I might be. I haven't got a certificate to prove I'm sane. By the way, how do you do it?"

"Do what?"

"Spring out at me whenever I come through the door. Is it radar? Or practise? Or a high content of nosiness?"

"You've been drinking," accused the shaken woman. "You must have been or you wouldn't talk this way. I knew from the first moment I set eyes on you that you had bad ways. You're a flighty good-for-nothing. Let me tell you, this is a respectable house."

"This is a drab, dreary, cheerless house, Mrs. Lamb. And you charge an exorbitant rent. I know, I know, I'll be leaving first thing in the morning."

Up in her room, she regretted her outburst. Not her intention to leave; Mrs. Lamb's would never be a real home, but she shouldn't have let her goad her into losing her temper. She should have explained. But how could she tell it without living it again, and it was too much to be expected to play the tragedy a second time round.

Her case was packed in readiness for the morning, the correct amount of rent sealed in an envelope addressed to Mrs. Lamb. She ought to sleep for a while. She didn't know why she couldn't sleep. Sleep would take this weight of thought from her mind and in exchange give her a few hours of peace.

Something wouldn't let her. A niggle, a thought. Some thing, a small something. A small . . .

She sat bolt upright, shivering, clutching her knees, remembering. Shari had said 'I came up to town to arrange a dental appointment for my small daughter.'

Oh, she'd really done a good night's work. She'd invited a young woman to her death, hoaxed a man in the cruelest way possible (Tony Martindale would never, never forgive her for masquerading, even unintentionally, as his sister) and, most poignant of all, orphaned a little girl.

A child who had learned to live

without a beloved daddy (surely every little girl's heritage) and must now adjust to not having a mummy either.

Who would look after her? Tony had said his and Shari's parents were dead, so no maternal grandmother was going to step in and try to fill this unfillable gap. Presumably the task would fall to his uncle's wife, who, according to Tony, already had enough on her plate with her husband's illness.

Her mind was a pumpkin of floating thoughts and disjointed ideas, inseparable companions skipping across the surface. Then a tiny seed of an idea broke away and settled in perhaps the only lucid corner; it took root and grew into a splendid thought. She took it out and examined it from every angle for flaws. But it was perfect, just perfect.

Why shouldn't she offer to look after Shari's small daughter? If she could be a solution, even a temporary one until they set their house in order, she mightn't feel as bad. It wouldn't absolve her guilt, nothing would, that was a blight, a shadow she would have to learn to live with, but if she could help . . .

They must let her help. True, she didn't know anything about small girls, but was there a lot to know? You tied ribbons in their hair and helped them make daisy-chains. In spring, of course, when the aprons of grass frothed a frill of those tender, pink-hearted flowers. Didn't you?

Sleep didn't come to Tony Martindale, either. He tumbled the bedclothes for perhaps an hour, then got up. He had been close to his sister. As soon as he cleared his head of this brain-dulling numbness he knew he was going to feel very badly indeed. He didn't bother to put on the light, but went unerringly to the well-stocked cocktail bar in the living-room and poured himself a drink. When Shari couldn't sleep it had been her way to make tea; his palate savoured the burning taste of whisky.

A knock sounded on the door, hardly a knock but a soft, persistent tap. He had to put the light on to see the clock. It was barely seven. Incuriously — what the hell did it matter who was there! — he went to answer it.

"Hello," said his visitor. She was muffled to her chin in that same sheepskin coat, fiery tendrils of hair escaped an emerald-green wool cap that was chic enough to happily grace the ski-slopes of Europe's most fashionable winter playground. Her mittened fingers nestled round the handle of a pale cream suitcase.

"Hello," repeated Sharon uncertainly. She hoped she hadn't got him out of bed and was relieved, then alarmed to see the glass in his hand. Relieved because she hadn't dragged him from his warm bed, his need for a drink could shoulder the blame for that; alarmed because after that first incurious second a dangerous look leaped to his eye. She couldn't tell whether he looked villainously drunk or just plain villainous.

"Having breakfast?" she said brightly. His: "M'm?" was both question and unsociable grunt.

"I was referring to the liquid refreshment in your hand." Surely he was going to ask her in?

"What do you want?" No, obviously he wasn't. Miserably she asked:

"May I come in?"

"What for?"

"If you'll let me in, I'll tell you."

"Fair enough." His brow was still tightly drawn, but he allowed her to enter.

"You're in," he said pointedly.

"Yes, well." She licked her dry lips, averting her eyes to take in the room, because he hadn't bothered to throw on a robe and it embarrassed her to stare fixedly at his pyjama-clad form. The tiny entrance hall was only a step away from the living-room. The colour scheme was autumnal. Men did, she thought irrelevantly, tend to favour the bolder hues. A café au lait rug edged a bitter-chocolate hearth where a coal-fire-effect heater supplemented the flat's central heating system. Berry-red and holly-leaf green cushions were tossed at careless angles on the tobacco-brown sofa; a seascape, magnificent and turbulent dominated the one white wall. It was a room which hadn't just come about, but on which a wealth of imagination and unstinting thought had been lavished.

And Tony Martindale was still waiting for her to explain, and it was too late to acknowledge the butterflies in her stomach. A bold approach and no smarting under that hostile stare and one, two, three, here goes:

"I'm sorry to disturb you, Mr. Martindale. Except that I haven't have I? I mean, you are up, just as I knew you would be."

"You knew?"

"Yes, I'd an idea you wouldn't phone home the," — she faltered slightly — "the sad news. I knew you'd want to go personally and I thought you'd want to make an early start. So, here I am to prepare your breakfast. A proper breakfast."

41

"Oh no, that's not the reason you came."

"It's not?"

"No. You didn't come here to burn your fingers on my breakfast bacon." It wasn't her fingers which were burning, but the tips of her ears, and all because of the way he was looking at her.

"Though what you did come for — ? Oh, I think I see. Did I forget to pick up the check? Let me see, services rendered: hand-holding, metaphorically speaking, of course. I don't know how I would have got through the evening without your support. However, I don't know the rate of charges for that particular service. Will a fiver be enough?"

"Don't be insulting."

"Yes, that is a bit of an insult, isn't it. Because of course you're playing for much higher stakes. You see, I too have been doing my arithmetic. But one thing puzzles me. Why did you phone me last night?"

"To . . . to . . . " She had come

42

this morning to offer her services as a nursery help, and also to make a clean breast of things. To tell him why his sister had been hailing a taxi and where she was going. But any confession needs to be levied in an atmosphere of sympathy and understanding, not one of suspicion and distrust. So, at the eleventh hour her tongue substituted words and she stammered: "To tell you I forgot to post the letters." That was perfectly true. Shari's disturbing telephone call had pushed everything else out of her mind and the letters she had worked at so determinedly, hadn't stood a chance of catching the evening post because they were still on the desk.

"I can check you know." The descending line of his mouth accelerated into a sneer and she felt sullied and defamed and she didn't know what was at the bottom of his ragged hints.

"Do," she thrust back at him, and all the fire in her hair leapt into her voice. Reason told her to say no more, but reason wasn't the driving force that made her add: "What's this? The M.I.5?" And she was crying inside at her own stupidity because the natural follow-up was to sweep haughtily out of his flat. And she couldn't very well do that and convince him what an admirable nursemaid she would make for his niece.

Oh! It was going all wrong. Why did she have to fly at him like that? Why couldn't she be sweet and even tempered and let her eyes plead her cause. They might be farther away from her heart than her tongue, but they were more in tune with its feelings. She didn't want to quarrel with him. That was the last thing her heart wanted.

"Well?" Translated that meant 'Why don't you go?'

Then, for a thoughtful moment he did look into her eyes. It was still unprepared ground. To ask anything of him now would be on a par with building a house and then looking where to put down the foundation. But this was probably her last opportunity.

"I thought . . . that is, I only want to help."

"Help?" He gave her a puzzled look. "How can you help?"

"Well, you are going to break the news to your aunt and uncle as soon as you can."

"Okay, I'll give you that. I'm going to Swallow Heights this morning." She presumed that was the name of the house and said:

"Please take me with you. I won't hold you back, or anything. I don't have to go in to work, I've written out my notice. I don't even have to go home to pack. I've got my suitcase here."

"I noticed. And wondered," he admitted, and she read the shadow of a twinkle in his eye and knew that if they'd been on friendlier terms he'd have made some joke about what happened to young ladies who arrived at his door at this impossibly early hour, complete with suitcase. As it was he said:

"I still don't see?" Something good happened. He didn't look angry any more, and his mouth even inclined towards a smile.

"Well," — deep breath and in with a wallop. "I thought I might be able to look after your niece. You mentioned yourself that auntie has enough on coping with uncle."

"Yes, I did mention *that*." His face was as smartly wiped clean of smile and indulgence as if it had never been, and immediately she saw the trap she had fallen into. Because of course he hadn't mentioned the child. Shari had. She wished, now, she'd been brave and told him about the telephone call. It was unbelievable that one small omission could cause such havoc.

Three normal strides separated them. He took each one slowly and she had time to taste the panic bubbles as they rose to her throat. They stood so intimately close that she could see the stubble on his chin and a tiny filling in one of his teeth.

"I didn't say anything about a child."

"But you must have," she bluffed. Her heart was slamming like a sledge hammer and it was her horrible fancy that it had little to do with the menace of his tone and everything to do with his nearness.

"How else could I know of her existence?"

"That is precisely what I should like to know," he said coldly. "But I don't for one moment imagine that you are going to tell me. So please go."

His teeth were clenched and he seemed to be holding himself in severe check. Sharon thought bitterly that he always seemed to be trying to get rid of her.

When her feet didn't match up to his command, he shrugged his shoulders and said with teasing indifference:

"Please yourself. But I'm going to get dressed."

She saw the rippling of biceps as he stripped off his pyjama jacket, and fled.

3

SHE could picture Aunt Lucy saying: 'Well, you have made a proper hash of it, haven't you, girl?'

'Yes, Aunt Lucy.'

'I shouldn't have listened to you. I should have whisked you off to Australia with me, and made sure you kept out of trouble.'

'Yes, Aunt Lucy. Except that you didn't want me to come to Australia with you.' Now she was cheating. It was wrong to say things in imaginary conversation that you wouldn't say to the person's face. And she would never have dared to say that to Aunt Lucy.

'You've changed, Sharon. I don't know what's come over you. You've let me down. I should have thought the influence of my upbringing would have produced better results.'

49

'Yes, Aunt Lucy.'

'But I shouldn't blame myself. The trouble is I didn't get hold of you soon enough. An impetuous nature like yours wants stamping on right at the beginning. My poor dead sister has a lot to answer for. But enough of that. I'm not one to speak ill of the dead. What was I saying?'

'You were saying I'm a disappointment to you.'

'And so you are. A sad disappointment.'

'I'm sorry. Aunt Lucy?'

'Yes, child?'

'What am I to do?'

'Do? Do? I don't know what you are to do. I know what *I'd* do.'

'What would you do, Aunt Lucy?'

'I'd forget it. That's what I'd do, child. Forget it.'

Forget it. Turn the little knob in your mind to forget. Don't think. Sit on a park bench and eat up your egg sandwich. Feed the scraps to the birds, watch them peck up the crumbs. Treacherous to think, except about impersonal things. What do you know, it's stopped snowing. Always a nice impersonal topic, the weather. It snowed yesterday. How it snowed yesterday! But she mustn't think about yesterday.

Here comes old blackbird, in a chirpy mood this morning, his beady eye on the last crumb. How cold everything looks, cold and bleak. Inside everything is cold and bleak, too. It's no use.

One last try. Then I will forget. I will make myself forget. Into the phone box. Quickly, quickly before I lose my nerve. Dial the number. Hear again the voice of the gravel-throated receptionist:

"Sorry, Mr. Tony is not in at the moment. He will be in later in the day, Madam. Say, around four o'clock."

So it was to be a quickie visit. Of course, he'd have to get back to see to things at this end. Was the idea born then, or had it been lurking in some inconspicuous corner of her mind? Certainly, words slipped off her tongue with the effortlessness of a carefully prepared speech.

"Actually, it's Mr. Valentine Martindale I wish to speak to."

"But Mr, Valentine hasn't been in since his illness."

"Hasn't been in?" Sharon's voice washed high in question, then ebbed in careful confusion. "I don't understand. Oh, perhaps I do. Don't tell me I've mixed the two numbers up again. That is Swallow Heights, isn't it?"

"No, Madam. This is Bonbon House."

She clicked her tongue. "How foolish of me. Sorry to have been a nuisance. I wonder, before I ring off, if I may trouble you further. Could you let me have the number of Swallow Heights? To save my looking it up in my little book."

"Certainly, Madam," obliged the nice receptionist. "It's Weatherford 992."

"Double nine, two," said Sharon. "Weatherford?"

"That's correct, Madam."

"Well, thank you. And goodbye."

Yes, thank you very much. But, what now? Telephone Mrs. Martindale? No, speaking on the telephone was a bit like saying your prayers. In faith, you spoke blindly, and without the visual link-up it was impossible to know what kind of an impression you were making,

Mrs. Martindale wasn't God, and Sharon decided she wanted all the clues she could get. Besides which, a curt 'No' over the telephone would have to be accepted, whereas if she was actually there pleading her cause there was always the possibility of a first hasty decision being rescinded. And she so desperately wanted to help.

If only it hadn't happened. If only she could have yesterday back to play again. But the cards had been shuffled and the hand had been dealt. A chill slid over her, and on to the screen of her mind flashed an impression of a pair of luminous eyes in a pinched little face. She wasn't a psychic person, which didn't mean she had never listened avidly to tea-leaf readings, but that she had never felt herself pushed by any presence she couldn't explain. Until now. She had to look after that unprotected motherless child. Motherless yes, but unprotected?

What a silly notion. The pressure of her thoughts reduced steam, the pulse in her finger-tips stopped drumming quite so palpably and she could even laugh and deride her colourful imagination.

All the same, she couldn't see any harm in making the trip to Weatherford and trying her luck with the aunt. To arrive after four o'clock, by which time Tony should be safely out of the way.

The rails sliced a true and straight course to Weatherford, and soon she was drinking in the soft country air and enjoying the uncomplicated admiration of the ticket collector, who she suspected was porter and guard and station master as well.

"Lovely day."

"Brrr . . . do you think so?" Casting an eye up at a sky as sullen and overladen as ever.

"Last fling," he prophesied optimistically, holding out his hand for her ticket. "Mark my word, spring's only just round the corner."

"Lovely thought," she said as an icy wind licked the exposed triangle under her chin. "Can you tell me, please, the best way to get to Swallow Heights?"

His eyes registered mild surprise, then hers did, because he not only advised but organised: phoning for a taxi from his cubby-hole of office, asking, no insisting that she occupy her waiting time — the taxi driver was out on a call and would be at least twenty minutes — keeping him company over a pot of tea.

In her book, station masters came old and grizzled. This one was neither and it would have been so easy to leave the bromides alone and slip into conversation. She would like to have pumped him about the occupants of Swallow Heights, but if she satisfied her own curiosity, it would be unpardonable to retreat from the probings he would then feel entitled to make. And she didn't want to explain her reason for being here, especially so because it could well be a futile mission. Tony's aunt might not want to engage a nursemaid for her niece, and even if she did there was nothing to suppose she'd look favourably upon Sharon. She might prefer to do her own seeking and take unkindly to initiative. Well, she would soon know. The taxi, long, black, limousine class, rolled up.

A vivid first impression is always the best and longest lasting. Swallow Heights, unlike the migratory bird from which it derived its name, looked happy in its winter setting. The road climbed all the way, winding the last half mile up a private road. The sharp angles of some of the bends made driving a chancy business even in favourable conditions; on a snow rutted road with icy patches as shiny-smooth as a skating rink, it was an exercise in caution. Not that she noticed; she recognised the driver's competence and the car's ability to sit the corners, and with the knowledge of this combination tucked in the compartment of her mind that dealt solely with self-preservation, she was able to fully absorb herself looking for the house through the trees, all hung in white and sentinel still, deeply imprinting the scene with an aura of loneliness and isolation. Except in one part where the trees clustered close together, it was visible all the way.

Even so she was unprepared for the loveliness of Swallow Heights. Comparatively new, it had been built of local stone, so while it gleaned the advantages of recent day developments, it had a quality of age and staunchness and mellowed beauty. It looked so perfectly natural in its setting that one could almost imagine its saying 'Old Tree knows what it's barking about'. And, taking a leaf out of Mr. Tree's book, had put down roots. Only, houses don't have thoughts and roots, they have foundations. Architects have thoughts. The one responsible for Swallow Heights had particularly good thoughts.

A spear of sunlight, the first she had seen in days, slanted down on the roof and glanced in at a window. She got out of the car and optimistically paid off the taxi-driver. Even if her mission was unsuccessful she wouldn't mind the downhill walk back.

As the taxi wheels crunched snow again, her eyes danced through the trees and down the road she had so recently ascended, to the roof of the railway station, and over to the left, a haphazard collection of roof tops cradled in the valley and which must be Weatherford.

She stood for a moment in the benevolent golden light of late afternoon, then took the four steps leading up to the front door at an impetuous rush.

Her eye collected details of the inside later, on that occasion it merely gathered an impression of good taste.

She thought briefly it must be nice to have the means to indulge and develop an eye for beauty, without suffering guilt pangs. Money, so far, had come to her on a tightly drawn line, the result of hard work and endeavour. As a result she tended to think before lashing out on something that was bought solely for adornment.

It was rapidly approaching the misty-purple hour; too early to draw the curtains and switch to artificial lighting, and yet the deteriorating daylight was unequal to its task. Shadows hung in the deep alcoves and in the folds of the long, golden velvet curtains. She had been shown into this delightful room, with its invitingly deep, relaxing armchairs, by a woman in her mid-forties, whom she took to be the housekeeper. Lovely room, dignified, remote, a stranger that might or might not open its arms to her in warmth and acceptance, but at the moment was reserving judgement. She had to strain her ears to catch the friendly and companionable sound of the ticking mantel clock and the hissing of the open fire.

The hairs on the back of her neck separated and lifted to pinch her skin, as if her neck was suddenly exposed to a draught, but in reality it was nature's special warning system, commonly called 'That uncomfortable feeling of being watched'.

Because she had supposed herself to be the only occupant, she was more relieved than startled when one of the deeper shadows jumped from the curtain to spear, and halve, the soft wedge of light falling in at the window. She had already accepted the fact that someone was there and the confirmation that this was so didn't alarm her.

No, it wasn't that which made her mouth fall open in a gasp of surprise, but a hotch-potch of emotion, apprehension and memory all falling together to be sucked into a single imperious cry.

Yet, afterwards, she didn't know why she was so taken aback and it was disconcerting to recall the stupefying effect it had on her. Of course her preconceived picture of Tony's aunt was miles wide of the mark. She had assumed a face to justify the role of aunt and had painted in tiny age lines and, because maturity so often disapproves, a thinning and pinching of the mouth, and for good measure she'd added a spangling of grey to the hair.

The hair was spangled, all right, but with the satin-sheen one might find on a selected bunch of black grapes, and the face was milky-smooth with wide apart eyes of a very deep blue, darkly iridescent, reminding Sharon of the irises that had run rampant in Aunt Lucy's large and untended garden. The hand which came out to invite so light a clasp that the fingers barely brushed, was a trim accessory to the lissome loveliness of that youthfully svelte body.

Then Moira, the girl she had met as recently as yesterday in Tony's office, said in that same bored drawl:

"Do sit down. Then tell me what I can do for you."

4

IT WAS a shock to find that Moira
was Mrs. Valentine Martindale.
Sharon was glad to sit down. She
told herself it was the unexpectedness
of it that had knocked her sideways,
because really it didn't alter the
situation. She couldn't altogether disallow a compassionate thought for the
uncle. Poor man, as if a heart thing
wasn't enough he had to have a straying
wife! But that was his mis-something
or other: management or fortune. If
he had to marry a beautiful woman
who was younger than himself, then
it was most inadvisable of him to
fall ill. A bored wife, and one knew
instinctively that illness or incapacity
of any kind would bore Moira to
tears, was a susceptible wife, a wife
ready and more than willing to take
a lover. Really, it was no concern of

hers. What mattered, the one, the only thing, was that poor little girl. Now, more than ever, because she couldn't see Moira making the effort to console the bereaved child. Bereavement would bore her, too.

Somehow, she must rid her throat of its ache and ignore the baiting half-smile on that pretty pink mouth. As if its owner knew. Knew what? That she had seen something in Tony, something beyond his stunning good looks and colossal charm, and more, had even acknowledged the lightning force of attraction and had held fast to the frailest handrail of hope that he, too, might — Might what? Not detest her quite as forcibly as he seemed to.

"You . . . you're probably wondering why I'm here," she began.

"I'm sitting on the edge of my chair," said Moira with the driest of sarcasm.

"I've come because of Shari," she said.

Ironically enough it was Moira who

blanched and stopped aspiring to raillery and the type of harassing, satirical humour she was so fond of, and so good at. "You knew Shari?" And now all she excelled at was hoarseness and uncertainty.

"No," regretted Sharon, because from their brief conversation she had gathered that Shari would have been a worthwhile person to have known.

"But you said — ?"

"That I'm here because of Shari. That's not quite accurate. I should have said, Shari's daughter."

"Jennifer?" The eyes glazed over, bored again, indifferent.

"If that's the child's name. Look, I know about Shari — " The lovely face jerked back and just as a hot breath mists glass, a hot breath of something misted up the glassy expression in those magnificent blue-purple eyes. But what? Panic? Fear? — "About her so tragic death."

"I see." Now the look was overlaid with a chilling coldness.

The room was not cold, indeed the warmth from the huge fire lapped into every corner, but Sharon was brushed with the ice in that glance, and she shivered.

Moira's chin dropped and her incredibly long lashes fanned her pale cheeks. Lifting, they revealed nothing more sinister than the grief one normally associates with any sudden or tragic loss and Sharon was glad to dismiss the strange undercurrents, disallow perception and admit to, as she always did on such occasions, a too keen imagination. Anyway, she was tired of groping with things she didn't understand and it was a relief to believe that what had disturbed her was non-existent and this was a normal reaction.

On cue Moira said: "*That* was dreadful." She drew in a telling, shivery breath, and Sharon's shoulders relaxed against the rich upholstery.

"Was it instantaneous?"

"I believe so."

That was something. She had once seen a dog run over. It had writhed in agony for ages before a vet arrived on the scene to put it out of its misery. It was a spectacle she never wanted to witness again, and one she could not bear to associate with a human being, "I'm not very good at offering condolence. But I am sincerely sorry."

"Thank you. It was good of you to call."

Sharon realised she was on the brink of being dismissed, that the moment was fast slipping away from her and she hadn't yet put forward the reason for her visit. She must beg a few more minutes of Moira's time.

Time: a moment in which things happen, absolute, inexorable things no entreaty on earth can prevent. Just as no earthly hand can stay time, hold it back, rub it out as if it was a badly recorded message on a tape.

"Wouldn't it be nice if life was recorded on a huge tape and we could rub out all the bits we didn't like," she said thoughtfully, forgetting for a moment that Moira sat in an opposite chair, pursuing her own thoughts. Thoughts that ran on remarkably parallel lines because she assented all too quickly:

"Yes that would be nice. Life does hold certain passages that would be better erased."

"Which is why I'm here," said Sharon. "I can't erase my bad passage, but at least I can make small amends in the only way I know how."

"I don't see — ?"

"I want to look after Jennifer."

"You?"

"I know it sounds preposterous. I haven't any qualifications, but could you get a proper nursery nurse at such short notice? You will need someone to help out."

"We have already discussed this matter and have arrived at a solution."

She stopped to give Sharon a speculative look. But Sharon didn't need that look to cringe, she was already aware that she'd said too much, had as good as admitted to a personal involvement.

"What passage of life would you wish to erase?"

Oh! the relief with which Sharon latched on to the mocking intonation, because Moira sounded as if she had sorted out any doubts she may have had, deciding, probably, they were panic ones and had reached the conclusion that Sharon was guileless, meaning harmless, enough.

"Dear me," she said. "What an intense girl you are. It's flattering that you should be so concerned and I appreciate the thought. But is it workable? Are you free of obligations?"

"Yes."

"You could start immediately?"

"I've got my belongings with me."

Moira's: "Really?" was followed by a "No, no, no," too vehement to be truly convincing. She sounded as if she was cancelling out an equally forceful 'Yes,

yes, yes.' And Sharon hadn't uttered a word. So therefore, she must be arguing the point with herself. It no longer seemed so cut and dried and conclusive.

"I'm tempted," admitted Moira, "but I wonder why you want this job. And if you really know what it entails."

"I don't. Not really."

"I thought as much. When you do know, you might not be as interested. How old do you think Jennifer is?"

Sharon pondered. She hadn't thought in terms of years. Shari had said small daughter, and she'd thought in terms of pearly baby teeth and a tot's mini dress showing half an inch of frilly knicker leg, and bows in hair and sugar-mice in plump, sticky fingers.

"Three? Four?" she hazarded.

"Twelve," said Moira.

Three, four, needed a nursemaid; twelve, attending school, didn't.

"I see I've wasted your time," said Sharon preparing to rise.

"No," said Moira. "After school

70

there is a need for someone to be in attendance. To supervise homework, ration television and see that bedtime is adhered to."

"Hardly a full-time job," pointed out Sharon. "Surely your housekeeper could oblige?"

"In isolated households such as this, housekeepers are cosseted, not asked to oblige. Anyway, Mrs. Pattern already has more than enough to do. My husband's illness has caused a considerable amount of extra work, Shari was a boon. She never minded giving Mrs. Pattern a hand; washing up, running errands, and she was always willing to entertain my husband, alleviate the boredom, as it were. She spent hours reading to him, cheering him up just by being there. The sick-room atmosphere, so distasteful to some, didn't seem to bother her. Not that my husband is an invalid now, of course. Do you understand?"

Sharon understood that this was a very different proposition from the one she had imagined, but was hers for the taking. However, the edge of her enthusiasm was definitely blunted. An imp of four or thereabouts, was well within her scope; the thought of an imp of forty or more, jellied her knees.

Moira was looking a shade anxious. A clip of conversation came back. We have already discussed the matter and have arrived at a solution. It didn't need a clairvoyant to know what that solution was. Moira would have to step into Shari's shoes, give up her job at Bonbon House, miss the daily grind which is meat and drink to a dedicated career woman. Yet Moira, however much she had beautified that executive-type desk, didn't strike one as a dedicate. So it was something else she was reluctant to give up. Daily contact with Tony, perhaps?

"Though why anyone should choose to hide away in this remote spot — What have you done? Fallen in love with someone unattainable?" She couldn't resist chancing the taunt, even though it was so patently obvious Sharon would be doing her a favour if she accepted the position.

"If it's not a man," she mused, enjoying herself, "there's really only one other possibility. You must have been instrumental in murder."

"Joke," she said, as all the colour drained from Sharon's face. "I'm merely saying it's strange. I'm not exaggerating, it *is* terribly remote. There's nothing at all in the way of entertainment."

"I'm not looking for a gay social life."

"You won't get one." Spoken very drily. "So take your time. The decision is yours."

But was it? Hadn't it already been made by an impulsive invitation and a car's tyres skidding helplessly on an icy surface.

5

'I HOPE you know what you are doing, girl.'

'Is that you, Aunt Lucy?'

'How can it be me. I'm on the other side of the world in Australia. You're talking to yourself.'

'Probably. That's because I've nobody else to talk to. It will be better now the funeral's over.'

'Yes, funerals are beastly. I warned you. I told you to stay out of it. But you wouldn't listen to me. You knew best. You young things always know best. Never listen to a well meant word of warning. Talking of warnings, I should watch him.'

'Him?'

'I understand your perplexity. I could have meant Tony. But I mean the uncle. Valentine Martindale is a damned attractive man.'

74

'Really?'

'Don't be coy with me, young lady. I've seen you looking at him. I've seen him looking at you, too. By the way, wasn't that a bit cowardly of you?'

'What?'

'Hiding away in the kitchen when Tony came. He must know you've wheedled yourself in, by now.'

'Not necessarily. I'm sure this family doesn't gossip at domestic level.'

'Nonsense! All families gossip at all levels. Anyway, you'll have to face him sometime.'

True enough. He'd looked in only briefly on the day of Shari's funeral. Sharon had thought it diplomatic to keep herself closeted in the kitchen, out of sight. Eventually, he would come to Swallow Heights for a longer visit, a weekend, perhaps. As she couldn't hope to shut herself away for a weekend, she would have to face him. That thought filled her with both terror and delight. She wanted to see him, to find out if this pins-to-magnet attraction was real and not something the romantic side of her imagination had made up. Yet she was terrified of what he would do. He had so totally misunderstood her desire to help and had fiercely resented what he considered to be an intrusion.

And that phone call when he'd thought she was Shari! Well, anyone would have smarted, but his hostility seemed to stretch beyond that. It was as if he had something against her, something she didn't know about. She did know that when he found out she was here, he would be murderously angry.

'I don't care. Whatever happens, I'm not sorry I came. Mrs. Pattern, the housekeeper, says I'm a big help.'

'Naturally. Even if I didn't manage to teach you restraint and obedience, at least I taught you how to keep a house comfortable and tidy and how to put on a good table.'

Cooking an appetising meal was one thing, getting anybody to eat it, another. Sharon sighed. It wasn't a happy time to be settling into a household. She was trying to do it unobtrusively, not forcing her presence. Everyone seemed so listless. The television was switched on, but nobody viewed. Eyes stared unseeingly. Jennifer's were always red-rimmed.

'Aunt Lucy?'

'M'm?'

'You still there?'

'I've told you before, I'm not here at all. I'm just a figment of your imagination. But don't let that bother you. Do go on.'

'What do you think of Jennifer?'

'Not much.'

'Aunt Lucy, that's uncharitable. What do you mean?'

'I mean, she doesn't let herself be summed up. She only talks in monosyllables and every time anybody addresses her she rushes off to her room and locks herself in. I think it's unnatural and unhealthy.'

'And necessary. Don't you see she's coming to terms with herself, with the situation she has found herself in. She'll come round in her own good time.'

It was grief that was making her withdrawn and uncommunicative. Sharon was certain of that. Neither plain, nor pretty, her face was still moulded in the contours of childhood. Although a hint of steadfastness was just beginning to show in the firming of the chin. Her thick dark hair was clubbed at ear level. She was built on athletic lines and Sharon thought she probably excelled on the playing-field. But her limbs moved listlessly about the house. And when the tears rushed, they did so in private.

Nobody saw, save perhaps Emmeline, the doll that had been banished to the back of the cupboard and had only recently been restored to favour. She combed its hair and fingered its dress and whispered things into its ear.

"You there, Sharon?"

Sharon levered her elbows off the draining board as the housekeeper entered the room.

"Yes, here, Mrs. Pattern."

"Alone?"

"Yes."

"I thought I heard you talking to someone."

"Only myself. It's a habit I seem to have got into. I'm sorry."

"Don't apologise. I do it myself. If you don't talk it out, it gets all warped in. I've just been trying to dig Jennifer out. Strange to see her playing with dolls. I almost said again, but that would imply she used to play with them and, in truth, she didn't. She wasn't a dolly-girl. More for skates and action toys."

"She isn't playing with dolls now," said Sharon. "Emmeline is a link with the past and she's drawing comfort from her."

"M'm, that sounds logical," agreed Mrs. Pattern. "Twelve's a damnable age to lose one's last surviving parent."

Sharon could have said 'Yes it is' with conviction. Because she had been twelve when she lost hers.

Mrs. Pattern was saying:

"Too young not to know, to old to appreciate what it's all about. There, I'm talking like a sage and making myself feel all morbid. Anyway, it's time for Mr. Martindale's afternoon cuppa."

"Shall I take it?" offered Sharon from force of habit.

She checked the contents of the trolley before taking it in. Sugar, biscuits; on impulse she added a second cup, thought 'perhaps not' and put it back on the shelf.

Since his heart operation, Valentine — although she called him Mr. Martindale to his face, she thought of him as Valentine — had occupied a downstairs suite of rooms consisting of bedroom, study-cum-sitting-room, and bathroom. Moira slept in her old room upstairs. They seemed to live separate lives. Sharon didn't know if this was from choice or necessity.

She found it hard to believe he had ever been under the threat of death.

She had to keep telling herself he was convalescent, that he had recently undergone a major cardiac operation that ten years ago was as out of reach and as ridiculously far-fetched as the idea of sending a man up to the moon had been to our forefathers. If it had happened to him ten years ago he would be dead. Certainly not grinning appreciatively at her over the rim of his newspaper, stretching out his long slim legs and injuncting her to fetch another cup. Sharon told him truthfully:

"I had the same idea. And before you."

He said an idea was no good unless it was followed up. So Sharon followed it up by fetching herself a cup and pulling herself a chair nearer to the trolley.

"Tell me about yourself, Sharon," he invited.

"There's nothing to tell."

"What do your parents think about your taking us on?"

"I haven't any parents."

"Who have you got then? Everybody has somebody."

"I have an Aunt Lucy. But she's on the other side of the world. And truthfully, I don't think I ever really had her."

"That's very sad." He said it as if he meant it.

She noticed he'd drained his cup and asked him if he'd like a refill. He said no and she topped up her own. She wondered what he thought about her coming here. If she hadn't come, Moira would have had to give up her job. Did he mind his wife working? Would he have preferred her to live at his slower pace and if he'd bought a house in the country earlier, slowed down a bit sooner, would it have made any difference to his health? She had heard one or two of the weird details of the operation from Mrs. Pattern, but still she didn't pretend to understand the whole of it. She wondered if he knew about Moira and Tony.

"Would you like to trade thoughts?"

he asked suddenly.

How truthfully she said: "No."

"All right. All right." He grinned amiably. "I'll trade my thoughts for the answer to one question. Any good?"

"Depends," she prevaricated.

His glance was conjectural, if lazy. "Why should a beautiful girl waste time on a broken angel?"

"I'm going to sound terribly vain answering that one," she said, "because I must assume I'm the beautiful girl. Then I must protest that you can't be a broken angel."

"I can't?"

"No. Because you're not broken, you're on the mend. And you would hardly qualify for the other. Angels are good."

"Aren't I?"

"Oh, yes. But a proper angel is good because it wants to be. Yours is a temporary goodness. I mean, you have to be, don't you?"

"In other words, you are suggesting I'm good because my wings are clipped," he said and there was a wryness in his voice and smile. Simultaneously a bomb of thought, two bombs actually, exploded in Sharon's brain. One, she was enjoying a flirtatious conversation with her employer, a man exactly twice her age. Two, the very nature of his operation demanded grave respect, and she was treating it as if it was not a barely escaped tragedy, but a very amusing joke.

Well, now she was sober enough. The colour ebbed from her cheeks, quick repentance drowned the humour in her eyes and her throat dug up a small abashed voice, one it hadn't had cause to use since the time she craved forgiveness from a very irate headmistress.

"I am sorry. I should never have said the half of it. I'm certain it's an appalling breach of etiquette. In future I will try to remember my place."

He stopped making a steeple of his hands and his eyes whipped up to hers; at the same time his throat tightened round the gravest tone ever.

"Then I can only hope you fail."

Sharon floundered. The ill-matching of tone and meaning threw her, and it was a full minute before it began to signify.

He amplified: "It's nice to be treated as an ordinary run of the mill being. A welcome change from being awarded the awed reverence of someone who has," — He paused, choosing between two phrases — "had their lease of life unexpectedly renewed."

Ordinary? Run of the mill? Never!

"So please, no apologies for thinking of me as a man."

A man, oh yes! very much a man. Not a broken angel at all. But a king among men with a king-sized personality that could easily surmount the limitations and temporary restrictions of his body.

He had a special sort of power. Everybody covets it, few possess it. It's called charm, although it frequently travels under other names and guises;

it's really the power to make a woman feel cherished and warm and madly interesting. He did it by forward-tilting his attention and letting the flattery flow freely from his eyes. He made no bones about liking what he saw. She wasn't a mirror hanger but she knew without vanity she was worthy of a second look, but she also knew that even if she'd been plain it would have made no difference and he would still have looked at her as if she was the most enchanting being on earth.

His face slipped into momentary repose, his mouth was trapped in the lightest grip of melancholy, and she wondered how Moira could risk hurting him. How could anyone hurt him?

6

'**D**EAR Aunt Lucy,' she wrote. 'I'm in love . . .' Her attention slid away from the sheet of notepaper and focused on her simple but elegantly furnished room. It wasn't a bit like a domestic help's room, one imagined that to be cramped beneath the roof, but more like a very important guest room. She sat at the writing bureau which she had pushed from its corner position close under the window.

Delightful as her room was, it couldn't hope to compete with the view. The road zig-zagged and twisted, a long silver snake whipping closely to the trees yet only once completely disappearing from sight so that any car, or pedestrian for that matter, turning up the private road was visible to anyone watching from the front of the house for practically all of the time. No one ever arrived unexpectedly because their approach was seen a long way off. The bendy road was less treacherous now that the snow had gone, melted by the sun or blown away by a gusty March wind.

She collected her wandering thoughts and looked determinedly down at the scrappy beginning of her letter.

'Dear Aunt Lucy, I'm in love,' She picked up her pen and added, 'with a house. I've completely fallen under the spell of Swallow Heights. I do hope you like Australia and that it — '

A light tap on the door diverted her attention.

"Come in." she invited. Her eyes went too high, this was because Mrs. Pattern was the only one who'd had cause to search her out. She lowered her glance, but not too far because Mrs. Pattern was short in stature and Jennifer was tall for her age.

A red exercise book was clasped dramatically to her breast.

"Do you know anything about algebra?" she asked without preliminary.

"Homework?" queried Sharon sympathetically.

"M'm. This subject's just not me."

"Me neither," admitted Sharon ruefully. "I could never remember when to change the signs from plus to minus and vice versa. But let me look, anyway."

Gratefully, Jennifer thrust forward the exercise book. "Miss Brown says my maths are going to let me down."

"Miss Brown?"

"My form mistress. She doesn't take me for maths. She takes me for History and English. I love history. It's like delving into people's private lives and their not minding one bit. Of course, they're all dead, aren't they, or p'raps they would object. I mean, it's colossal cheek to want to know how many wives a man had, with Henry in mind."

"And how he disposed of them," put in Sharon. "I never thought of history as permitted nosiness, but I suppose it is. I wonder if that's why it's such an intriguing subject, because we can pry without being thought impertinently curious. What other lessons do you like, Jennifer?"

"English. Miss Brown nearly always reads my essays out to the class."

"What do you write about?"

"People mostly. They fascinate me. I like meeting someone new, someone I don't know anything about. I invent stories round them and work out in my mind how they'd react. When it's real and alive inside me I put it down on paper."

"I wonder what you've plotted round me," said Sharon. There was just the faintest suspicion of amusement in her voice. "I hope I acquitted myself well."

Jennifer looked doubtful. "You didn't come out too badly, if that's what you mean."

"That's exactly what I mean. I'd like to think I kept cool and was equal to whatever faced me. But I suspect that's just a wild fancy. I bet if it came to it I'd go to pieces and be a terrible liability to whoever was on my side."

"I don't think you would," said Jennifer loyally. "I'd like us to be on the same side." Her voice was so wistful Sharon wondered if there was a situation, or if the child had caught herself up in her own embroidery. Without thinking she said:

"Love, if you don't make the grade writing, try the stage." That earned her an aggrieved look and she found herself biting on her lip and thinking this poppet is too sharp by far.

"Miss Brown says some of the things I write are good enough to be published and, if I work at it, there's no doubt in her mind that I could be a successful writer. She says I have tender insight as well as imagination. She says a lot of aspiring authors have one but fall down on the other and, therefore, never make their name."

"Is that your ambition? When you grow up, do you want to be a writer?"

"Oh, yes," she said, her prickliness

91

of a moment ago blown away on a breath of sharp ecstasy. "I love making up stories. I do it all the time. It's natural, like breathing. I don't think I could ever stop, so it would be lovely to get paid for something I'd do anyway, and for nothing."

Sharon wondered who, or what, had navigated the conversation into less dangerous channels. Chance? The child's guiding star? She wasn't old enough to have acquired the complicated art of licking words so effortlessly into shape, despite Miss Brown's premise. She conceded:

"You have a point there, Jennifer. One must have a healthy respect for money, after all it's essential to have it in order to live, but far too many people select employment solely for its remunerative advantage and spend a third of every working day doing something they hate. Which brings us back to your algebra. Sticky, isn't it? Who usually helps you, if anybody?"

"Uncle Valentine. He's terrific. He

knows all the plus and minus rules and how to transpose and everything."

Sharon heaved a sigh of relief and suggested without guilt, and only marginal shame at her own scholastic shortcoming:

"Why not ask him, then?"

"I did think about it. But I didn't know if I ought to. He's been under a terrible strain you know, with the operation."

"Yes, I did know."

"And Mummy said — " It was the first time in Sharon's hearing that she had made reference to Shari. Her guiding star failed her and in the space of a second she changed from an exceptionally bright, near-brilliant twelve year old, into a shaking, bewildered little girl. She tried to stop the silly tears by tightly clenching her fists and screwing them in her eyes. But this only made her hands wet.

Sharon watched, feeling useless and inadequate. Bereavement was such an acute and personal thing that she never quite knew how to handle it, even when dealing with adults. And Jennifer seemed too young to be so totally bereaved. So very young. It no longer seemed absurd that Shari had given Jennifer the tag of small daughter, simply because she wasn't small in her mind. If you lose your footing on one of the lower rungs of a ladder, you haven't far to fall, but if you've aspired to heights, probably before you are ready, the fall is greater.

A twelve year old with tender insight is especially vulnerable to hurt and pain. Shari would know all about that, of course.

Quite suddenly, Sharon knew what to do. Simply and effectively her arms went round Jennifer and she said inconsequential things into her ear. She didn't know what it was all about and couldn't put a name to it, although it was probably maternal something or other, but it felt comfortable and natural and Jennifer was able to mop up her tears without loss of dignity.

"Sorry. Didn't mean to turn on the waterworks."

"That's all right. Have you a hankie?"

"No."

"Take mine."

"Thanks."

Though Jennifer's smile was too slight to press the dimple in her cheek, her mouth was less tremulous.

"You were saying?" prompted Sharon.

"Well," gulped Jennifer. "Mummy said we mustn't bother Uncle Valentine with our problems. She said we mustn't say or do anything that could possibly cause him anxiety, because we wouldn't be able to live with ourselves if we were the ones to set him back. She said that although he was so well, he still had a long way to go."

Sharon said gently: "Helping you with your homework won't set him back. Solving mathematical equations is a tease, but not a worry. Your mummy didn't mean that sort of problem."

But something acute and urgent. So urgent that she had defied weather conditions which were so appalling that even long distance lorry drivers, who took practically anything in their stride, postponed or waited it out in friendly, noisy transport cafés.

She had said she had come to town to arrange a dental appointment for Jennifer. But was that the truth or a quickly thought up excuse? She could have made a dental appointment with less expenditure of effort. All she had to do was lift up the telephone.

No, it was definitely not that which had caused her to venture out, but the problem. Whatever it was she daren't risk bothering Valentine because he was going through a period when relaxation and freedom from worry was the best medicine he could get. Yet, had she bothered him she might be here to tell the tale.

"Jennifer," said Sharon impulsively. "If anything troubles you, anything at all, will you promise to tell me about it straight away. No matter how absurd, I want you to promise you'll come straight to me."

"Anything? Even murder?" said Jennifer shooting her a keen, alert look.

Sharon worked hard to keep her expression on an even keel, though her mouth desperately wanted to widen in a gasp.

"What do you mean, murder?"

"Nothing. I didn't mean anything."

"I think you did."

"But you won't take any notice. You'll say I've made it up; just because I'm good at making stories up you won't believe me. And even if you do you'll say it was an accident and not murder."

"Try me. What will I say was an accident?"

"Being run down by a car." The set of her young lips, the angle of her chin, pleaded with Sharon not to mock. As if she could, with that memory burning like acid into her conscience, because that spur-of-the-moment invitation had served as a death wish. Because Shari had accepted she had been run down by a car.

"It was on the third bend," said Jennifer, leaning over to point out of the window.

"What are you talking about?" Sharon also craned forward to look at the access road to Swallow Heights. The third bend was the one screened by trees, the only part of the road not visible from the house.

"The third bend. That's where it happened. That's where she tried to run me down."

"She?"

"Moira. It was a Tuesday, which is my day for going to the Guides. I was so very nearly home that she must have seen me from the house before she set off, and yet she came swooping straight at me like a bat in the night."

"You don't like your Aunt Moira much, do you?"

"No."

"That's why you're making up this horrid story. You are making it up, aren't you?"

"Am I?" she taunted in that dramatic tone she achieved without effort. "I knew you wouldn't believe me. But I had to prove it."

Chilling, daunting words, because it was instinctive to disbelieve so absurd a tale. Later, Sharon was going to remember this and be chilled afresh, chilled and horrified and beside herself with frustration.

Because the truth is often absurd. Because people won't believe.

But then, in sublime unawareness, her mind pondered on Jennifer's gift, ability, call it what you will. If only she wasn't such a talented story-teller. And what did she hope to gain? Did she think her wild imaginings would erase the hurtful reality?

"You are a silly goose," said Sharon, hugging her with sympathetic understanding. If she was behaving badly, who could blame her? "Anyway, it couldn't be murder, because you're still here."

"That's right," said Jennifer, and that saucy dimple pressed wickedly deep. She picked up her exercise book, darted Sharon a look that said very plainly 'Thanks for nothing' and left the room.

Sharon stayed by the window, staring out, morbidly fascinated by that bit of road obscured by the trees. She thought it wasn't only algebra that confused and puzzled her.

"Aunt Lucy?" she said. But there was no reply.

7

SHARON came to the conclusion that it was her own keen imagination that was making her receptive to Jennifer's embroidery. Even if there had been a car incident, which she very much doubted, it could have been one of those near-scrapes, a stupid miscalculation of judgement, nothing more.

It was a comfortable decision to arrive at because she couldn't believe Jennifer's story and not do anything about it. And what could she do? Who could she tell? Not Valentine, who was making such marvellous progress. He could climb stairs and go for walks and he was even toying with the idea of renewing his golf-club subscription. Like Shari, she had no wish to be the one to set him back.

Shari had turned to Tony. Or tried

to. Sharon wished she could. He had a nice solidness about him, a sort of dependability. She'd been foolish to antagonise him. But she hadn't, it was the circumstances she found herself in which had. The trend of those circumstances froze her thoughts; just as Wednesday is for ever destined to follow Tuesday, there was a frightening inevitability about things. She felt too uncomfortably at home in the role she was playing, as if she had auditioned for it long, long ago. So long ago, in fact, that she'd forgotten a vital point, something she ought to remember and act upon. She recalled Jennifer's words. 'I just knew you wouldn't believe me. But I had to prove it.'

That's how she felt, as if she ought to set about proving something. But she didn't know what.

What, exactly, did she know? She knew that Shari had raced to town in a terrific panic. But she didn't know why.

But Jennifer did. Her thoughts stabilised,

stopped right there. It was uncanny how she knew that Jennifer knew this thing that had worried Shari; knew it, even if she couldn't properly understand it. She couldn't explain why she thought this way, it was one of those instinctive certainties she would be prepared to stake her life on. And if she knew, with the pitiful little she had to go on, mightn't someone else? Someone who might not want it, whatever it was, made common knowledge, and might have reason to want it suppressed . . .

She didn't think beyond that point; progressive thoughts were too frightening, too numbing. But every day just before four-fifteen, which was the time Jennifer arrived home from school, she found herself standing guard by the window, watching for the first glimpse as she turned up the road.

She wore one of those long scarves that were all the rage, twirled round her neck to bob below the neat hem of her brown regulation, school gaberdine. The scarf was bright red, not regulation, and spent the day ignominiously stowed at the bottom of her satchel, hidden by the bulky presence of her English textbook. Her form mistress would certainly have disapproved, but Sharon wholeheartedly approved. It bobbed, like the red robin in the song, all the way up the twisty road, beautifully visible.

Once, Sharon waited for the school bus to drop Jennifer off. She had been to the shops for an ounce of plum coloured wool and a packet of adhesive plasters for Mrs. Pattern, and several items for herself, including a flashlight. It was flat, shaped to fit in pocket or handbag, yet with a fairly powerful beam for raking dark corners. She didn't quite know what dark corners she meant to rake, but she felt comforted by its purchase. On reflection, it would be handy if she woke up in the middle of the night and didn't want to switch on the bedside lamp. Or for walking up the access road in the dark.

So far she hadn't ventured out after dark. At first she hadn't minded the lack of things to do, but several times during the past week she had caught herself in the act of nostalgically remembering visits to the theatre or cinema, or her favourite discotheque. Then she asked herself 'What's a fun-loving girl like you doing in a place like this?'

The bus wasn't late, Sharon was early. Yet she experienced a feeling of keen relief as she spotted the bus and Jennifer, near the door, waiting to alight, the flying ends of her scarf bobbing up and down, matching her impatience.

Now, Sharon would have been prepared to swear on oath that it was Jennifer, but what she recognised was an identical coat and scarf. The face that looked up belonged to Patricia Mason, whose mother was nearing her time (Jennifer's wording when later she explained her friend's presence on the bus) and so she had come to stay with her grandmother, who lived in the village, until after the event. Jennifer, whose slighter form had been obscured by the larger one of the butcher's wife, leaped off the bus after Patricia. Sketching her friend a cheery goodbye, she linked her arm companionably through Sharon's.

"I shall be late home, tomorrow," she said. "I got a detention."

"Bad luck," sympathised Sharon. "What for?"

"For telling a lie and being impudent."

"You?" It didn't fit. Jennifer wouldn't consciously tell a lie. Although her powerful imagination might stray perilously close to the boundary line of truth. Which must have been what happened. Neither would she mean to be impudent. But, poor pet, with that saucy dimple she'd only to effect a half-smile and she was in dead lumber.

"I didn't tell a lie," said Jennifer with the same stubbornness that had got her into trouble. "Miss Brown told us to write an essay. We could choose our own subject, but it had to be based on fact, something that had happened to us personally or to someone we knew. She said mine was very good, but she couldn't give me any marks because it was so obviously fictitious. I said it wasn't. It was fact. It had actually happened."

"Needless to say, you didn't convince her."

"No. I realise now I should have accepted her decision. But no marks at all, it seemed so unfair."

"So what happened?"

"She ticked me off for being impudent. Guides Honour, if it was I didn't mean to be. I only wanted to make her see I was telling the truth."

"Instead of which you landed yourself with a detention. Never mind, sport."

"But it's so unjust. Honestly, I could scream."

"I know. There are times when I feel that way myself."

"But you're grown up."

"Yes."

"Grown-ups can't give way to their feelings. It must be dreadful to have to bottle things up," she speculated.

"I wouldn't know," Sharon could say with truth. "I'm a blower, not a bottler. Sometimes I wish I had a nice even temperament."

"It wouldn't go with your hair," pointed out Jennifer prosaically.

"Then I wish I had mud-brown hair to match. It's horrible to be labelled."

"I know," said Jennifer with feeling. They'd gone away from the subject, travelled round in a circle, and come back to it. "I'm labelled imaginative and people instantly think everything I say is made up."

Sharon's understanding nod prompted Jennifer to say:

"Did you ever get a detention for something you hadn't done?"

"Frequently. You know how some people are accident prone? Well, I'm reverse situation prone. By that I mean I always seem to land myself in a

108

situation which isn't what it seems. The facts say one thing, when really it's not that at all."

Jennifer was wrinkling her nose and saying: "Y-es." And Sharon was conscious of drifting into deep waters and yet not knowing how to paddle out. Now they were approaching Jennifer's third bend, the spot where the house was hidden from them, and they were hidden from the house. Earlier it had rained and raindrops quivered from every leaf, spraying them fitfully with fat jewel drops. Sharon opened her mouth to say something, saw Jennifer's frozen expression, and checked. The child really did believe that Moira had tried to run her down on this spot. For anyone with murder on their mind, it was ideally placed, screened from the house and the road below. Nobody could see . . . without a witness, nobody would believe.

"That time . . . " Sharon passed her tongue over her dry upper lip. "Was Moira alone in the car?"

"I don't know. I don't even know if it was Moira."

"But you said — ?"

"Yes. But since then I've had another think. It was what you said about things not always being as they seem. I think it was Moira's car. I sort of assumed it was Moira driving, but I can't be sure. You see, it was very dark and we were momentarily blinded by the car's bright headlights."

"You said we," said Sharon excitedly. "You weren't alone? You had a witness?"

Jennifer's: "Yes," was basic, without joy or triumph, a flat monosyllable that named the witness more poignantly than words.

"It was — Mummy."

"The car didn't stop, then?"

"No. We half sprinted, half jumped into the hedge. Mummy said the driver didn't see us, or probably thought we were rabbits scrambling for safety."

"That's what you must believe, Jennifer."

"I do. That's what I believe," she said, but her face wore its hurt, closed look again.

After that disturbing conversation, Sharon wanted more than ever to get away from Swallow Heights. Not permanently, but just for a few hours. It would be bliss to relax in an atmosphere that wasn't electric, to be able to re-charge as it were, or maybe just be able to sort herself out so that she could reason between what was real and what was pure fantasy.

She was sitting in the window corner of the drawing room, her nose in a book. She didn't hear Valentine enter the room and he was standing on top of her before she realised she was no longer alone.

"What are you reading?" Before she could answer he took the book out of her hands, read the title on the spine, then shot her a surprised, amused look. "I thought such absorption would merit a sensational spy-thriller, at least! Instead of which — "

"Algebra," she said for him, tilting him a sheepish grin.

"You do take your work seriously, don't you?" he said.

"M'm, I suppose I do. I don't like anything to beat me."

"Tenacious, eh?"

"Yes. Although I'm not terribly keen to admit to it."

"Why? Don't you consider tenacity a virtue?"

"No. Sometimes it's better to let go. Of an idea, of a person."

"Any particular idea or person in mind? Or are you generalising?"

It was his tone that caused her cheeks to redden.

"Oh, my gosh! I didn't mean anything. It was just something to say."

Truly, she'd forgotten the odd state of his marriage. The only thing he seemed to share with Moira was indifference.

"That's all right. I know my marriage is on the rocks. It shook me to know it's obvious to a comparative newcomer."

"Is it?"

"Is it what?"

"On the rocks?"

"All but. Don't look so shattered. I'm not."

"Is there a how or a why? Oh!" Her hand shot up to her mouth. "Don't answer that. It's too dreadfully impertinent."

"I'm not touchy on the subject," he assured, so obviously striving to put her at ease. "I wouldn't mind answering, if only I knew the answer. If there is a reason, it doesn't come to mind. We never quarrel. We're never in the same room long enough to quarrel."

"Perhaps that is the reason," said Sharon very softly. His hurt, the emotion he was bravely covering up, was her hurt.

"Yes, well," — he was the first to break free — "that's enough about . . . about an uninteresting old recluse."

Uninteresting? Old? Recluse? No, no, but *yes*. Did he hate being a recluse?

Did he miss the hectic, active life he had so recently lived? Thinking of life recently lived, her own, she said: "Are you, by any chance, familiar with the bus times? I thought I might go out one evening, to the cinema or something. That is if you don't object."

"Object? What makes you think I might object?"

"Because you're frowning."

"Yes, I am," he admitted. "It should have occurred to me that you'd miss things. What sort of things do you miss."

"All sorts of everything," she said with a twinkle. "Cinema queues, rush-hour traffic. Having my feet trampled on on a tiny square of dance floor."

"Ah yes!" His sigh was as nostalgic as Sharon's own. "Dancing. I haven't danced since . . . " He shot over to the radiogram, plugged it in, selected a record, fitted it on the turn-table, came back to Sharon an idiotic smile parting his lips. Strains of dreamy dance music, the old fashioned kind that made her

114

think of last waltzes and handkerchiefs smelling of lavender, filled the room. Laughingly she accepted the invitation of his open arms and they danced round and round, threading expertly between the furniture.

"Better than algebra?"

"Much better."

He pulled her into a spin as the music died.

"Shall I put it on again?"

"No."

"'fraid I might tire myself?"

"Yes."

His arm was so lightly, so casually round her waist that she wasn't conscious of it until she saw Moira standing in the doorway, and then the palm of his hand and all five fingers burned into her skin, but the flame was in her cheeks.

"Don't stop on my account," drawled Moira. "So pleased to see you are finding your . . . dancing feet," she taunted.

Sharon cast a hasty glance at

Valentine, expecting him to be furious. But he was smiling pleasantly enough.

"I'm considering putting in an appearance at the firm's dance."

"That's good," said Moira indifferently. "Don't you think so, Tony?"

Sharon jumped a mile. She hadn't looked beyond Moira, but now she took in Tony's long form lounging against the door jamb. He cocked an eyebrow at her as if to say 'Hello, it's you. So you managed to wangle yourself in after all.' There was something interrogative about the curve of his mouth, a half-formed 'Why?'

Clearly and achingly she remembered their last encounter. Then he had been stiff with anger. Now he looked relaxed and almost amiable. Nothing had happened in the interim to make him feel differently towards her so she could only assume that she, personally, hadn't been the cause of his savage mood, but that he had been raw with grief at losing his sister and that had angered and embittered him. Then, remembering again the details of that night, she shivered. She guessed that he and Shari had been unusually close even for brother and sister. Even when she knew him better, would she ever be able to confess the secret of that night?

"Moira has just asked Uncle Val if his burst of energy has taxed him. Strangely, you are the one with the pallor. Are you all right?"

That was Tony, unsmiling, yet solicitous.

"Yes, thank you."

"You dance well," he said.

"Thank you. It's something I enjoy doing."

"I also. Have you ever been to the Grove Hotel?"

"No, but I'm going."

"Oh?"

"Well, after that build up, you are going to invite me?"

"You're an impetuous creature, aren't you?"

"Aunt Lucy says it's my nature."

"Aunt Lucy is probably right. Aren't you afraid of getting out of your depth?"

"I try not to think about it. Well, are you asking me out?"

"Of course."

"When?"

"On second thoughts I like your impetuosity. It's flattering. This evening?" His smile of enquiry didn't just crust the surface but cut deep, knifing a way into his voice so that she too felt strangely flattered, and yet at the same time she was conscious of a tingle of unease. They'd parted as enemies and met again as friends. The transition was too abrupt for her to adjust. Anyway, she didn't know if she feared him more as a friend than as an enemy.

They'd kept their voices low and this created an illusion of aloneness and there was, therefore, something poignantly shattering in the way Moira's hand fluttered to tug at Tony's sleeve and her voice was at once soft and harsh. Like emery paper rubbing on silk.

"Tony, you're not dashing straight out? I've just told Mrs. Pattern to set an extra place at dinner. She hates being mucked about." The indelicate phrase sounded odd coming from her tongue; she was so beautifully cultured in manner and speech, unnaturally so and almost to the point of being an exhibitionist. Yet even as Sharon lapped up that catty thought she had a feeling that Moira's irritation was justified. But she was a married woman, so how could she rightfully lay claim to his time?

"I'll fix it with Mrs. Pattern," said Tony, quelling her with a look.

"Yes, Tony." She was unnaturally submissive. Why?

The evening had started off benign, unseasonably warm, but as darkness fell the temperature dropped and the road curving away from Swallow Heights was starry with frost; the inside of the car was as warm as summer and she might have felt snug and relaxed if Tony hadn't been sitting so close. It occurred to her he couldn't move, but she could. She shuffled nearer to the window, ignoring the thought that it had been nice to have his shoulder sitting tight against hers every time they went round a bend.

"Comfy?" His tone, dry and amused, told her he was aware that she had moved. And why. Especially the *and why*.

He knew he was a dangerous element. She wasn't lulled by his apparent friendliness. But curious. He hadn't changed course without good reason. She shivered.

He startled her by saying: "Cold?" Because surely her apprehension hadn't shown.

"No. Beautifully warm, thank you." He was sensitive to her every movement. Tuned in. She didn't like that. She preferred her telepathic wires to be crossed. She didn't like being read.

He concentrated on his driving and,

after a while, her thoughts turned back. To Moira. Her attitude was a puzzle. With Tony she was melting sweet, a willing Aphrodisian puppet ready to jump when he pulled the strings. Well, perhaps she could understand the power — attraction — he had over her, but she was hanged if she could understand why Valentine let him get away with it.

On reflection, perhaps she could. He'd undergone a difficult operation and until he was fully recovered he needed Tony. The business needed Tony. Until such times as he was able to take command, Valentine had to put up with the situation.

She thought she would have preferred bankruptcy. But then, she didn't know how deeply, how emotionally he was involved. It looked like a business to her, but she hadn't seen it reared from a recipe, a thought, an idea. It might be life itself to him. *Poor* Valentine.

What a deplorable position to be in. She couldn't condemn him. But she could condemn anybody mean enough to take advantage of a sick man. And she despised herself for melting towards Tony. For losing that fragile shell of aversion and turning to him, despite herself. For admitting in her inner heart that she'd never enjoyed herself so much.

Yet who could fail to enjoy such a wonderful, memorable evening. It was almost as if he knew of all the tension she had to shed and was doing his utmost to help her. He was even more charming than usual, although on reflection she had no yardstick to measure what usual was, so perhaps this was Tony. Sweet, wholly fascinating, laughing at her over the top of his apéritif, giving the intoxicating impression of sharing something, perhaps just happiness.

Students of human nature have been known to compare life with a stage. Anyone who knows anything about stagecraft, knows that all important plays — and the play of life must surely qualify — must have peaks. Well, so had their evening, and that moment was peak number one.

Peak number two came after they'd eaten delicious, expensive food in the lush atmosphere of the Grove Hotel and he owned to a compulsion to dance with her. His compulsion nicely coincided with a trill of sweet tremolos, and as they swept into a waltz she silently thanked the management for tucking this type of dance in between the modern ones more usually favoured by her age-group.

No dialogue here, just a movement so perfect it would have gladdened the heart of a top-line choreographer. Their eyes met in unspoken admission of a truth she found too palpable to put into words. If she was in a seventh heaven just by being held in his arms on a dance floor, what heights would she reach if he made love to her! Then she wondered if his attentive eyes could read her thoughts and a wave of scarlet poured into her cheeks, and to her dismay stayed there even when the music faded.

She fanned herself with her handkerchief, and then she was being led out on to the balcony. The Grove Hotel just had to have a balcony, and steps leading down to a sunken garden which in summer was pretty with rock plants and night scented stock and fairy lights twinkling in the trees. But now it was gnarled shapes and a cold wind singing against hot flesh. And peak number three was here before she'd time to realise or prepare for it, although she had only to look round at the trappings to know that any director worth his salt would have earmarked that moment for a kiss.

A crescent moon silvered the tips of the taller trees soaring above them, ambitiously trying to pin the night sky. Kind trees that chaperoned and would never tell and drew them into deeper shadow so that the light lancing from the tall french windows opening on to the balcony, cut only a sword of light across their feet.

She shivered without knowing why. He asked her if she was cold and she said no, but all the same he removed his jacket and solicitously wrapped her into it.

"Now you'll freeze," she protested. "It's . . . it's *freezing* weather."

Whenever she was nervous she repeated herself and tended to prattle inconsequential things.

His laugh was dry. "Darling, this is no time to talk about the weather."

Now, now, now, sighed a baby breeze that surely ought to have been tucked up in bed hours ago. Now, now, *now*.

His kiss was direct and sure and determined. Not at all like the imaginary kiss of her dreams. That had been hesitant and tender. More of a 'Please may I?' than anything else, and her lips had quivered, warm and tremulous under his, answering 'Yes, yes, *yes*!'

How different was the reality. No

granting of favours for the simple reason that none were asked. His hands didn't play innocently with the escaping tendrils at the nape of her neck, but roughly assaulted her shoulders until she was forced against him in undignified surrender.

She was a prisoner to his desire, then her own; this in spite of herself because she was willing her lips to remain lifeless. It was too humiliating to respond to this 'grab what you can, while you can' high handed treatment. Humiliating, degrading death to a girl with pride and spirit, sweet enervating death that hungered for the continued sweetness of possession.

The air smacked cold against her lips. Now that his mouth had left her mouth, his eyes fixed on her eyes. His expression was strange and unfathomable.

"So! Just like the rest of them, you're willing to pay your corner."

The raw sarcasm in his voice was like a whiplash.

"I . . . I don't know what you mean."

"Come off it. Of course you know. I might be highly susceptible, but I'm not stupid. I know you didn't just happen to me. You've been planted on me for a specific purpose and I shan't rest until I find out what it is."

"Tony, please . . . I . . . " Her voice broke. If only she had the courage to tell him. But she had! She'd never in her whole life shirked an unpleasantness. So why didn't she tell him?

Jennifer was why. Jennifer needed her. If she told him about speaking to Shari on the telephone and being responsible for . . . what happened, he would be angry. So angry he would make them send her away.

"I'm sorry, Tony. I can't tell. Please . . . please don't ask me."

"All right. I won't spoil tonight."

Fatal to ask, but: "What's special about tonight?"

"You . . . you are! My warm, lovely, desirable darling. This is one of the perks, I suppose." His mouth had softened, now it hardened again.

"All the same, I can't help wondering how far you're prepared to go to keep me happy."

She thought quickly. "As far as the dance floor. You must be blue with cold."

He shrugged wistfully. "Perhaps you're right. Happiness is many things. At the moment it's a warm pair of hands and feet."

8

NEXT day, Moira gently quizzed her.

"Did you have a nice time yesterday evening?"

"Yes, it was very pleasant, thank you." Polite, cagey words.

"What do you think of Tony?"

"He's all right," she replied guardedly.

"But not your cup of tea?"

Only one answer to that. "I like coffee best."

Moira simpered. "Good. I think we understand one another."

Sharon realised, without affront, that she'd been warned off. She sighed nostalgically. In the not so long ago if a couple didn't hit it off, at least they made a pretence. Nowadays, only the die-hards were prepared to stew in their own matrimonial juice; a growing proportion came to an agreement.

Sharon wondered if the agreement gave Valentine the same scope it gave his wife.

"Will you be coming to the firm's dance?"

"When is it?"

"Friday."

"I haven't been asked."

"I'm asking you. You can keep an eye on Valentine. He insists he's well enough to attend, but I don't know . . . "

Poor Valentine, thought Sharon with rising irritation. 'Keep an eye on him' As if he's a small boy, a nuisance to be kept occupied while the grown-ups attend to their pleasure!

"I haven't anything suitable to wear," she said rebelliously.

"Who has?" said Moira with earthy logic.

"I'd need an afternoon off to go shopping."

"Don't ask. Just go."

"All right. I will!"

"Today?"

"Why not!"

Sharon was woman enough to enjoy her shopping expedition. Somewhere, deep down inside of her, was a thrifty streak. It usually won in such matters, but then, never before had it had to battle with such a forceful need to impress. Yet, trying to compete with Moira would be like trying to vie with the sun for brilliance and lustre. But just because she was eclipsed it didn't necessarily follow that she needn't make the effort. Yes, but it was possible to make an effort without spending an exorbitant sum on a dress that might be worn for just the one occasion. This self-argument continued right up to the moment she entered plate glass doors which hitherto she'd awarded no more than a cautionary, if envious, glance.

She brushed shoulders with mink and yes! — occasionally rabbit — and her senses floated and almost drowned in the conflicting clouds of perfume: light, heady, sweet, woody.

The dresses weren't on rails to

happily rifle through, but each one sat passively under its own protective cape, waiting to come to life under caring feminine hands, to delight and enrapture and draw cries of 'What an exquisite shade!' or 'How beautifully the material hangs!'

Velvets; silks and satins that gleamed like clear, still water and then rippled to life at the merest finger touch. As if to say, Look at me. *Do* look at me.

And what colours! a haze of pastels: blues, pinks, and the fragile green of a new-born leaf. Bolder hues: a lemon, acid enough to set the teeth on edge, turquoise and cobalt, a smarting-hot red and an impossibly fiery orange. And white.

Sharon looked at the green and the gold and squandered a few fruitless moments on the impossibly fiery orange. Some red-heads could wear this shade well, others at disadvantage. Sharon was in this latter group.

"I'll try on the white."

It was the least expensive of all

the gowns, yet it still strained her pocket and reduced her thrifty streak to near-hysteria. It was a beautiful dress. Nothing pretentious about it; just simple lines and exquisite good taste. She hoped she wasn't stepping above herself. After all, she was only a Martindale employee. Difficult to remember, when no one treated her like one.

She arrived back to find Moira's car parked at a sloppily careless angle in the drive. Her first thought was, that's unusual. This because Moira was by nature a precise sort of person; it was almost a fetish with her to leave things straight: books in bookcases, newspapers neatly folded, reels of thread with the ends secured in their little notches, cars in drives. Something must be preying on her mind to make her so careless.

Sharon's second thought was condensed into a single:

"Goodness!" Because either Moira was home early, or she was later than she had supposed. No time to take a peep at her new purchase, she deposited it on the bed and scuttled back down, meaning to help Mrs. Pattern with the dinner preparations. But first she bobbed her head round the drawing-room door.

"Mission successful and all present and correct," she told the back of Moira's head.

"Oh, Sharon." — Spinning round — "Don't just stand there. Come in." Not something wrong, but something *drastically* wrong. Her face was as white as if it had been dredged in icing sugar, and her hands nervously twisted a book-mark. A leather one, scarlet, inscribed with a gold windmill. It belonged to Jennifer.

Sharon shook her head, shaking out irrelevancies. She always noticed the unimportant things. She thought if I witnessed a smash and grab, I wouldn't take a note of the get-away car's registration number, but I'd be able to tell them the culprit had a nice smile

134

and carried a light-weight raincoat.

"What *is* the matter?"

A voice, not Moira's voice, replied:

"Nothing. Nothing's the matter. It's all a storm in a teacup."

Sharon started. She had been unaware of Valentine's presence and, oddly, his voice jarred on an unfamiliar terse note. He was sitting in the same deep armchair she had sat in when she was first interviewed for her position. His face was half in frown and half in smile, and the frown was more real than the smile.

Moira said nothing and mutilated the book-mark some more. Jennifer had lots of book-marks, but the red one was undoubtedly her favourite. Sharon wondered how she could extricate it without apparently doing so.

Valentine leaned forward. "For goodness' sake, woman, take hold of yourself." For all the synthetic smile it was a command.

"Yes, Valentine."

"It's nothing. A slight delay."

"Yes, Valentine." The book-mark received another vicious twist.

"These things happen. There will be a simple explanation. You'll see. No need to let your imagination go into orbit."

"I'm sure you're right."

He got up, with leisurely indifference, and selected a pipe from the pipe-rack. He'd been advised to curtail, or give up entirely, cigarettes. Or at least cultivate a liking for pipe-tobacco. He viewed the pipe in his hands with extreme distaste. Pipe-smokers were born and not made. With a look almost of revulsion he put the stem to his mouth and sucked. Nothing happened and so he extracted a pen-knife from his pocket and began to poke at the barrel.

Moira put the book-mark down on the table. Sharon might have retrieved it then, but she hesitated for a fraction of a second and the chance was lost because Valentine addressed her and it would have been impolite not to give him her whole attention.

"What do *you* think, Sharon?" He sounded nice and reasonable. Perhaps he reserved that impatient, gritty tone exclusively for his wife. Perhaps her assessment was wrong. Perhaps when he wanted to he could stand up for himself.

"I don't know. I've only just come in, remember?"

"Of course you have, my dear. Well it's this. As you see, Moira's getting into an awful flap, and all because Jennifer is a *tiny* bit late home from school."

"A full hour," cut in Moira. "Even if she missed her bus she couldn't be *that* late. And stop making me sound like a neurotic," she said tardily. "I don't like it."

"If you don't wish to sound like one, then don't behave like one," he said, with a significant tightening of the muscles round his mouth. "I tell you there's a perfectly simple explanation."

"That's true," contributed Sharon. "There is."

137

She was the immediate focus of two pairs of eyes. One pair frankly disbelieving, the other pair, set higher and under thicker and heavier brows, set a puzzle.

"What do you mean?" enquired Valentine.

"I mean, Jennifer is late for a specific purpose."

"You know what it is, of course, or you wouldn't be so positive. Unless," The puzzle — his eyes, which suddenly held a faint but definitely hopeful gleam, and why should that be? — deepened. "I know, you're being beautifully kind. Considering our feelings?"

"I'm not being kind or anything. I really do know why Jennifer is late. She earned herself a detention at school. She told me about it yesterday. Obviously she didn't tell you."

"No."

"She must have forgotten. Perhaps I should have mentioned it." She was absolutely fascinated by the look in his eyes. Perhaps he didn't know how revealing and utterly transparent they were or else surely he would have guarded them, looked away or something. Now they were deeply apprehensive, displeased, more than a little speculative. And they were turned full on her.

"Yes, you *should*."

She shivered. It was harrowing to be so very much in the spotlight.

Moira intervened. Not by look or gesture, but by her spine-straight stillness. She was cringing away from what Valentine might say, and it was her very real and obvious fear which radiated the message 'Easy, my love.' Yes, her brittleness had gone and, for a split second, so short a time that afterwards Sharon thought she must have badly misconstrued, there was tenderness and a spontaneity of love, warm and outgoing and deeply compassionate. The tension eased. Valentine said:

"But never mind. After all, there's no real harm done." His heartiness dispelled the ghosts and she could laugh with him.

"I'd better give Mrs. Pattern a hand. She's usually glad of a bit of assistance about this time."

"M-m? Oh, yes." He replied absently with a mechanical lack of expression. He walked over to the side table where Moira had deposited the book-mark, brooded over it for a moment and then, to Sharon's horror, began to trace a criss-cross pattern across the gold windmill with the point of his pen-knife. He looked at it and said with quiet surprise:

"Look what I've done."

His amazement was genuine, his contrition absolute, and yet Sharon burned with anger. He thrust it forward and she accepted it, and looked sorrowfully at the roughed-up edges, Moira's handiwork, which she might just have been able to smooth out, and at the neat cuts, Valentine's, which were irreparable.

If she'd moved when she ought to

have moved, she could have saved it. She *knew* she could. Her fingers caressed the red leather. It had been so beautiful and perfect and she could understand why Jennifer treasured it so, and she hated violence and unreasonable, wanton destruction. Hated it and failed to understand how anyone could be evil enough or careless enough to destroy so utterly and completely.

It didn't occur to her that her feelings on the matter were ridiculous and quite disproportionate. Not until Valentine said:

"Don't look so tragic. After all, it's only a bookmark."

141

9

LIFE has a way of going smoothly and nothing happens, and the everyday sameness is, in its own way, as depressing as a burial stone. Or else it is not so smooth and things move at a feverish, hectic pace which is more wearing than the boredom. And, anyway, anyone with a bit of initiative can alleviate that but so far, for all the genius of man and his sprints round the moon, no one has been able to come up with something that can space happenings so that they come with regular, welcome breathers in between.

Sharon would have welcomed such a breather. She felt as if she was being rushed, pushed and made to feel both foolish and frightened by her unwelcome inheritance. That's how she saw it, a complex situation, an unwelcome inheritance that was showing a marked reluctance to reveal its secret.

The policeman, she looked at his unobtrusive grey suit and his feet, and she knew he was a policeman, came calling next day. He asked to speak with Valentine and was shown into the study, where the two men remained for twenty or so minutes before Sharon was invited to join them. Invited appears to offer a choice, whereas it was an imperative command, police-wrapped to sound like something as mild and obligatory as a request.

"Sharon," — This from Valentine — "Come in, my dear. This is Detective Sergeant Thompson. He'd like a few words with you. Detective Sergeant — Sharon Swift."

"Good afternoon, Miss Swift." His smile was polite, probing. He didn't extend his hand and so neither did Sharon.

"Just a few routine enquiries," said Valentine, so obviously offering comfort that she was touched. "Nothing to worry about."

Sharon wondered if she looked worried. She didn't feel it. This was her first contact with the police in an official capacity, although she had once been dated by a police cadet with a rather sweet smile. More to the point, Aunt Lucy had brought her up to respect the force and regard it as a staunch and reliable friend, to be called upon in times of trouble and need.

"That's right," mimicked the Detective Sergeant, "just routine." She felt that he might have smiled, the feeling of a smile was there in his eyes and about his mouth, if there'd been anything to smile about. Obviously it, whatever *it* was, wasn't a smiling matter, and she composed her own features into an expression of suitable gravity.

He began: "Does the name Patricia Mason ring a bell?"

"Yes, it does," replied Sharon without hesitation. "She goes to Jennifer's school. I believe she's a year or so older than Jennifer."

"Three to be precise. Small for her age, would you say?"

"Not really. I did notice the two girls were almost identical in height, but I put that down to the fact that Jennifer is tall for her age."

"When did you notice, Miss Swift?"

"Yesterday — no," she corrected, "yesterday Jennifer was on detention and missed her usual bus. The day before, then."

"You're positive?"

"Quite. I'd been doing some shopping in the village and by the time I'd got everything it was nearing the time for Jennifer's bus to arrive. So I decided to wait for her and we walked home together."

"And that's when you saw Patricia Mason?"

"Yes. She was the first to alight. For a second I mistook her for Jennifer."

"Oh? Why?"

"I don't know why. I haven't thought about it until now." Her brow crinkled in concentration. "I suppose my brain was conditioned to expect Jennifer, and so I saw her."

"A natural enough mistake," agreed her inquisitor, "especially as the girls were almost identical in height and wore identical school uniforms. I believe the regulation colour is brown and yellow?"

"That is so."

"I take it, then, that Jennifer doesn't break school rules to wear a hat with a pompom or whatever the current fad happens to be?"

"A scarf, Detective Sergeant. Red and practically sweeping the ground."

"What's that?"

"The latest fashion fad."

"I take it that Jennifer isn't a slave to this particular trend. Otherwise you would have identified her by the scarf."

"But she *is*," maintained Sharon. "And I believe that's what I did. You see, Patricia Mason is also a fashion slave. They both wore long red scarves."

"I see." A pause. "Just a thought. Wouldn't your brain have been conditioned to see two red scarves?"

"No. I'd never met Jennifer's bus before, but even if I had met her every day my mind would still have been conditioned to see just the one girl, the one distinctive scarf. Patricia Mason didn't usually travel on that bus. It was her first time. Jennifer told me so. Patricia had come to stay with her grandmother, in the village, for a while. But you'll know all about that?"

"Yes, I do. Actually, I was aware of most of the things you've told me. It's mainly a question of confirming every detail. Monotonous, perhaps, but very necessary in cases such as this."

"This?"

"Yes. Perhaps I should explain. Patricia Mason got off the bus yesterday afternoon. She hasn't been seen since."

"Oh no! Can't you do anything?" She felt fiercely, passionately concerned.

"I'm doing something. I'm taking statements."

"I mean something *useful*. Oh!" Her hands went up to her face. "I'm sorry, that was unkind and impertinent. But I feel so intensely. I think kidnap is the beastliest of crimes."

"Kidnap?" One eyebrow ascended, but otherwise he was as sluggishly placid as ever. "Who said anything about kidnap? We're treating this strictly as a missing person enquiry. We've no reason to suppose otherwise."

"You mean . . . you think Patricia has run away? But why?"

"Delicate age. I believe fifteen is an emotional turnstile in a girl's life. Delicate situation; only child, young adolescent. Apparently she resented the fact that her mother was pregnant. And now, I'll thank you for your co-operation and wish you good-day."

* * *

"It might have been me," said Jennifer dramatically. "If I hadn't got a detention I'd have been on that bus and I might

148

have been the one to be kidnapped."

"Don't be ridiculous," chided Sharon. "I've told you umpteen times, Detective Sergeant Thompson said there was no question of kidnap. Patricia Mason simply took it into her head to run away. Girls do, you know."

"Why?"

"I suppose because they're unhappy. Jennifer, do you think Patricia was unhappy?"

"Yes, she was *very* unhappy."

"About the coming baby?"

"Yes."

"How do you know? Did she talk about it?"

"No. She never said a word. That's why I know she was unhappy. I mean, if you're looking forward to something you want to talk about it all the time, don't you? But if it's something you dread, then you don't talk about it. You pretend it's not there and hope against hope that it'll go away. Personally, I think Patricia's daft. It must be nice to have a little sister, someone to talk to, someone who'll always listen and not put forward grown-up arguments. Do you have a sister?"

"No. I've got an Aunt Lucy."

"Do you talk to your Aunt Lucy?"

"I used to. But not any more. She's gone too far away."

"Did she listen to you when she was here?"

"Sometimes she did. Sometimes she didn't. Would you like to hear a comforting thought? Grown-ups are children who have learnt how not to be transparent. Some grown-ups never learn how to hide their feelings and that means they haven't properly grown up."

"Even if they're old?"

"Even if they're old. There are lots of sixty and seventy year old children."

"Is that the comforting thought?"

"No, this is. Some wise grown-ups have learned to hide their thoughts so well that when you think they aren't listening, that's when they're listening really hard."

"Thank you," said Jennifer primly. "That *is* a comforting thought."

* * *

Two days later it was Friday. Chores took up the better part of the morning. After the dance, Tony was coming back to spend the weekend at Swallow Heights, and Mrs. Pattern was glad of Sharon's help in preparing his room and performing the usual end of week tasks. In the afternoon she patronised Weatherford's one and only hair stylist, gossiped under Veronica's deft hands, the drier, and then again in the square. Still no news of Patricia Mason. She had been seen getting on the bus at the school gates, and getting off it in the square. After that she might have disappeared into thin air for all anybody knew.

It dimmed Sharon's pleasure. She couldn't conjure up any gaiety at the prospect of the evening ahead and would rather not have gone, but then she supposed so would a lot of other people. Betty and Edward Mason, Patricia's parents, had been and was, respectively, Martindale employees. Betty had worked in the packing department until two months ago. Edward was the chief wages clerk. Both were extremely well liked. Betty's eyes were said to moisten when listening to the misfortunes of others — who couldn't genuinely like a sympathetic listener in a world where priorities were going slightly askew and everyone wanted to be talkers? And Edward Mason was known to be a soft touch with a deep pocket. If the cause was worthy. He didn't suffer fools and people respected him for it.

A child is missing. It doesn't stop daylight coming or night falling, or the bit in between when the sun drops to the horizon and the sky is painted glorious, dramatic colours and one tends to forget that it's something to do with atmospheric pollution and sees only the flying snakes of red in a shimmering pool of gold, nature's own nightly spectacular. Simple, beautiful, effective, defying capture in prose or on canvas.

Sharon was almost ready. Her face was made-up and her evening bag and slippers were ready to be picked up or slipped into at the last moment. She had just slid into her dress when a light tap sounded on the door.

Help? It would certainly be appreciated. She opened the door. Her expectant smile turned into surprise.

"Oh! Mr. Martindale. Er . . . hello," she said awkwardly.

"Valentine," he said. "Please call me Valentine." He was smiling fatuously and holding two drinks. "May I come in? I knew you'd be ready. You're that sort of girl." To ask what he meant would, she felt, be courting disaster. To her relief he elucidated:

"Precise. On the dot. I thought we could have a drink together. To help the convivial atmosphere along. What's the matter? You could use a drink, couldn't you?"

"Yes, to drown my party butterflies. But — "

"I *see*," he said. He did see. He shooed her into the room, set the drinks down on a convenient table, and ordered her to turn around. His fingers found the little tag at the end and the zip of her dress negotiated a swift and true course up her back.

"Thank you."

"The pleasure was mine."

The service was performed quickly and impersonally, but still she felt a tingle of embarrassment. She wasn't used to exposing her naked spine.

He retrieved the two glasses from the table and handed one to her.

"I thought this might be a good opportunity to talk. Oh, I know we talk a lot, but never in privacy. As soon as we begin a conversation, that's the signal for someone to interrupt." That was very true. "I figured out the only way to guarantee a private conversation was to seek a private venue. I can't think of anywhere more private than your bedroom, can you?"

"No."

"Am I embarrassing you?"

"No. But my curiosity is burning. *Do* go on."

"Look, why don't we sit down."

"You may. My dress won't permit it."

"I *see*." He grinned and added mischievously, "I really do see. Very attractive. Cigarette?" He held his cigarette case out to her.

"No thank you."

"Mind if I indulge?"

"Not at all. But should you?"

"It's all right. I'm counting. I'm allowed this one and my next at twenty minutes to twelve."

"Do such restrictions bother you?" She softened towards him, as she always did at any reminder of his operation, of the bravery with which he had faced his ordeal. He lit up before answering and regarded her thoughtfully through a plume of blue smoke.

"Funny you should say that, because I was going to ask you the same question. Do my limitations bother you? I want you to answer that at a purely impersonal level. You know, as a woman."

"Very well. If you were half the man you are, you'd still be twice as good as the average male."

"That's very kind of you."

"No, I'm not being kind at all. You asked for the truth and I've given it to you."

"Would you have done so had the truth been less palatable?"

She thought for a moment. "No. How could I? If you were less of a man, if you hadn't come to terms with yourself and the situation you found yourself in, then it would have been, as you put it, a less palatable truth, But I wouldn't have told a lie." She smiled. "I would have been a trifle evasive. Explanation satisfactory?"

"Very. It encourages me to proceed

to question number two. Why don't you like me?"

She hedged. "Are we still talking impersonally, or do you mean me?"

"I mean you."

She wished now she had accepted the cigarette. With luck she might have choked to death and been saved the trouble of answering.

"I do like you."

"But not as much as you liked me to begin with."

King, devil, oracle, clairvoyant all rolled into one. He seemed to have at his command an infallible wisdom and unfailing knowledge. And enough charm to make one doubt the doubts. God is himself, the devil has to charm.

She thought: Of course, you are perfectly right, Valentine. I don't like you as much as I did at the beginning. I don't know why, because when you exert yourself you are a very likeable sort of person.

Could it be, she asked herself, that she was afraid of him? Not, strictly speaking, of him, but of his king-sized personality and the strange magnetism that flowed between them, a swiftly running current that only a fool would deny. A fatal attraction that wouldn't be flattened even though she stamped on it and trampled on it she couldn't grind it into the ground.

Ridiculous! It was only Valentine. She was frightening herself to bits and — she looked at him and saw that his eyes were round and bewildered. Childlike. Either she was going mad or he had a split personality, because one moment she saw a king, the next she was confronted by a bemused little boy. His lips seemed to tremble, as if to say 'Please like me.'

"I *do* like you," she said loudly and aggressively.

"Do you?" He perked up. "You've no idea how much it pleases me to hear you say that. You know, at one point, just before my operation, I didn't care if I lived or died. I'm glad I lived, if only to hear you say that."

"Oh, Valentine. Don't say more. I shall weep."

"Because of me? I'm touched, my dear. No one has ever wanted to weep over me."

"Surely that's not true. Moira? Doesn't she weep?"

"Oh yes." His eye dispassionately flicked the red tip of his cigarette. "She weeps if a dog loses an ear in a fight. Once she wept all the way through a film. I've thought of something. A possible reason why you don't like me as much as you did at the beginning. Is it the way I handle Moira? Do you think I'm harsh with her?"

"No. But even if I did it wouldn't trouble me, because I think she deals unfairly with you. But she is still your wife. Let's *both* remember that." Her words fell into a small unhappy silence. Then she said: "In case you didn't properly understand. I was asking you to go."

"What do you mean? Oh, I see!

If the mistress catches the master in the maiden's room. Sounds like a conundrum, doesn't it? You are a maiden, aren't you, Sharon?" Her hot cheeks told him she knew what he meant.

"Yes, I am a maiden," she replied woodenly, hoping he would soon go. Valentine was a stimulant to be taken sparingly. And to think, because of a faint family resemblance, she had once likened him to Tony. Tony would never play with her like this. If he had something on his mind he would come straight out with it.

"Maiden." He was enjoying himself. "You should read the dictionary's definition. It's quite amusing." He looked round for an ashtray, found one, and carefully stubbed out his cigarette. "Just now you mentioned Moira. Quite deliberately. Does it bother you that I have a wife?"

Instead of giving her time to answer, he went on to say: "It shouldn't. Neither Moira nor I make a pretence about our marriage. We're together because neither of us has the incentive to want to be free. You are a very moral person, Sharon, not the type to settle for second best. I understand that. I know there can be no future for us unless I obtain a divorce. If I did get one, would you marry me?"

"No, Valentine, *no*. I'm sorry." And wretched and apologetic for not knowing he was going to propose, for letting him humiliate himself. "I couldn't marry you."

"Oh. Is it because I'm a crock?"

"Valentine, you mustn't say things like that. You are not a crock."

"I know. I know. I wanted you to say it. I made you say it. I'm not a crock. I've been through a dreadful ordeal, Sharon, and I've triumphed. A lesser person would have cracked under the strain, you've said so yourself. I've proved myself."

She had a sudden sharp memory of an incident with her young cousin Simon. Years ago, on one of the many occasions she had been charged by Aunt Lucy to keep an eye on him, he had taken a tumble, skinning both his knees. 'I didn't cry, did I, Sharon? Any other boy would have howled like anything, wouldn't he, Sharon?' 'Yes, Simon. He would.'

"Yes, Valentine. You've proved yourself."

"Then why don't you want to marry me?" His voice held a surprised note of reproach. "I want to look after you, to cushion you, to protect you. I'm considerably older than you are and the chances are you'll be widowed fairly young. But that needn't be so alarming because my money will take over where I leave off. Money is a good protection, Sharon. You'll be adequately provided for."

"Valentine, please stop. I can't bear you to talk like this. If I loved you I wouldn't give a damn for the consequences, about your age or the future or anything."

"*If* you loved me?" He didn't merely

look surprised, he looked stunned.

"You mean you don't?" He couldn't imagine anyone not falling victim to his indisputable good looks and charm. In truth, she had fallen victim, she did find him a fascinating character, but dominating, enervating. She didn't know whether it was his strength or his frailty which wilted her most. She was only thankful she didn't love him because the effort to do so was more than she could contemplate.

"I'm so sorry."

"It's all right." He smiled. The brave little soldier right to the end.

"I hope this conversation won't make any difference to us. Just because you can't give me your love, I hope you won't withdraw your friendship."

"No, of course not."

"Will you prove it? Will you prove it by accepting these?" As he spoke his hand went into his pocket and brought out a small, jeweller's box. He flipped open the lid. On a pad of blue velvet rested two earrings. Gold, with tiny diamond drops. Neat, unpretentious, exquisite.

He saw the momentary leap of excitement in her eye, the longer-lasting warmth of appreciation, woman's natural reaction to beauty, the inevitable reluctance of her withdrawal.

"I couldn't. You know I couldn't."

"Why not?" He lifted one earring out and held it up against her ear.

"Yes, you could wear these. You have pretty ears. Why won't you?"

"You *know* why."

"No, I don't know why. Unless," — his brow tucked thoughtfully — "you think I'm trying to bribe you?"

"Aren't you?"

"No, I've accepted your answer. I want you to accept this gift as a token of friendship."

"I can't." Her denial sounded small and insubstantial. He could taste the thickness of her despair on his tongue. She shrugged her shoulders.

"I'm not trying to thwart you. I would have accepted a small token,

164

but not the earrings. They are far too valuable."

"Excuses, excuses." He was laughing inside. "I don't believe you. You won't do anything to make me happy."

"That's not true," she said wearily. "You're asking the wrong things of me."

"All right. I'll accept that. This is my third and final request. Will you wear them for this evening? To please me," he added as her mouth framed a no. With a sigh she changed it to yes. He made it impossible for her to refuse.

"I will wear them for this one evening," she said. "But you must promise me you'll take them back."

"I promise. I promise." She didn't hear the hint of jubilation in his tone. Her mind was too fatigued to pursue thoughts that would normally have assailed her. For instance: Why did he look as if he'd scored a major victory and not a minor triumph? As if this was the outcome he'd worked so desperately hard to achieve.

"Let me put them on for you," he said.

She acquiesced meekly. She hadn't the energy to refuse.

"So delicate, so exquisite." His finger and thumb imprisoned the lobe of one ear, then the other.

His mission was accomplished. Now he left. Unmindful of creasing her dress, she sank into the nearest chair. She hadn't wanted to wear the earrings. Yet how could she have refused him without being churlish. She felt wrung, emotionally and physically. And the evening hadn't yet begun.

10

THE earrings were as light as nothing. Normally she hated wearing earrings, finding them heavy and cumbersome, but these were so deliciously light she couldn't feel them. To make sure they were still there, she had to put a finger up to touch them, or catch a glimpse of herself in a passing mirror as she was danced round and round the ballroom.

At first she had wondered whether she would get any partners, but she quickly found out that Martindale employees were not cliquish and willingly admitted her into their midst.

Now that she'd had time to think over and properly assimilate the conversation she had had with Valentine, she could feel only astonishment that he had proposed. She wasn't knowledgeable on the subject, it was her very first proposal, but she thought a woman was supposed to know when a man's thoughts were bent on marriage. Didn't they look at you in a special tender way? Want to continually gaze at you, talk to you, smile at you, touch you? Yet Valentine had given no clue, hadn't betrayed himself by word, look or gesture. Of course, his marriage complicated matters; all the same, it was a miracle he had covered up so efficiently.

Her first proposal! She felt dreamy and — yes grateful! It gave her self-image a terrific boost. Even if she never received another it would always be there. She would be able to think, I had a *choice*. I could have been protected and cherished. I could have been Mrs. Valentine Martindale.

This thought had unfortunately coincided with the meeting up of the present Mrs. Valentine. Her foot was on the last stair when Moira and Valentine came out of the drawing-room. Shyly she avoided his eyes and instead looked at Moira. She hoped it didn't show, this new, smug, arrogant feeling, familiar to all newly proposed to girls. If it did she knew Moira would find a way to cut her down to size.

"Sharon, how nice you look. Doesn't she look nice, Val?"

"Yes."

Sharon looked self-consciously down at her feet: all the same she didn't miss her cue. "So do you Moira. You look ravishing,"

"Thank you." The heavy lids dropped and the head inclined. The compliment was received with such enviable panache that it frayed the edge of Sharon's satisfaction. She felt gauche and girlish in her white dress, even if it did cling in all the right places. This was because Moira's was more vital, more vivid. Pink, it had all the sour bite and sweet sharpness of a freshly picked raspberry: beautiful, subtle. With her figure and hair colouring the effect was stunning.

Now, appraising a wide variety of

females of all shapes and sizes, in an even wider variety of fashions, she thought Moira's nearest challenger was a tall willowy blonde, looking taller and more willowy in a colourful patterned silk trouser suit. Automatically she glanced at the girl's partner and what she saw burnt through the façade of her pretend enjoyment. Now she had no reason to look at every new arrival who came through the door. Now she could really come to life. Her spirits soared, sang louder than the group making happy mayhem, a disenchanting discord of sound that maimed the senses in the most delightful way, and invited a compulsive burn-up of energy. *Now* the evening could properly begin. The girl's partner was Tony.

I've lived twenty-two years without you, she thought. What a waste! How many years have you lived without me? She didn't know his age. She knew he was within his depth. He'd swam out of the young years, that awful toiling time of doubt and uncertainty and was — thirty? Plus or minus a year.

She realised she was behaving abominably towards her partner, a square fresh-faced boy, his face was as pink as a crab, of about her own age. He was trying so hard to prove himself an intelligent and amusing companion, and she was squandering her thoughts on a wretch who wasn't even looking at her. After that glance of acknowledgement, he'd bent to his partner, wearing a look of complete absorption.

She turned to her partner, building a protective fence round herself in a smile which grew, with only slight difficulty, into a laugh. Conversationally he'd just about dried up. It's hard, unremitting work talking to a shadow, not so when the shadow sparkles into a gay, attentive girl. It encouraged him to continue with the narrative, except that he couldn't remember what he'd said to make her laugh.

The music ended and she re-joined Moira and Valentine. No sign of Tony.

She saw him again four dances later. He was still with the blonde in the striking trouser suit. She didn't know whether he'd been with her all the time, or whether he'd danced with someone else in between. Preferably someone fat and unattractive and matronly.

The highlight of the evening was the Belle of the Ball competition. The Master of Ceremonies made the announcement over the microphone and invited the entrants to line up. The competition was open to Martindale employees only. Guests, that is the wives and friends of Martindale employees, were barred from entering. Senior executives, such as Moira, refrained from choice. This year, for the first time, Moira was one of the judges. The other two were Valentine and Tony.

"We really ought to be making our way to the judges' platform," fretted Moira, craning her neck. "Where *can* Tony be. Ah, here he is! You naughty boy" — pointing a playful finger — "where *have* you been?"

"Dancing. It's usual at this sort of function," he replied dryly.

"You haven't danced with me." — pouting attractively.

"Naturally not. I got all the duty dances out of the way first. Then I can concentrate on my own pleasure."

"Darling boy," said Moira on a different note. "On occasion you can be *so* charming. I forgot your dedication to duty. Have you danced with Sharon yet?"

Sharon was aware that his eyes were now fixed on her, carefully she averted her own, avoiding direct contact. No, he hadn't danced with her, and she wasn't ready to forgive him. Also she wished Moira hadn't bracketed her name with that remark about his dedication to duty. Valentine sent her a sympathetic smile, but she was too wrapped up in her own thoughts to notice.

She thought that Eris, the goddess of discord, must have looked as offensively self-complacent as Moira did now,

173

when she threw the apple among the guests at the wedding feast.

"Later," she heard Tony say. "I shall dance with Sharon, later." He said it in such a way as to indicate a pleasure deferred and she swallowed and smiled and the lump in her throat dissolved. But the apple of discord isn't such an easy fruit to swallow and, anyway, Moira hadn't finished with her yet.

"Why don't you enter for the Belle of the Ball?" she challenged Sharon brightly. "After all, as an *employee*, you are eligible."

Sharon thought it was mean of her to trade so blatantly on her own superior position, as if for a moment she needed reminding. In the circumstances she thought it was probably kind of Moira to say employee instead of servant, as the stress she put on the word indicated the latter. She thought to herself: Well, and so you are! So what's all the fuss about? Then she lifted her chin in sweet defiance. "I tend to forget I'm only a paid employee. That's because everybody is so kind to me, treating me as a friend, almost, if I may be so bold, a member of the family."

Tony's smile was barely perceptible, but it was there all right. Sharon thought he had a very self-disciplined face; she didn't envy him because she wrongly imagined her own to be as mask-like. Valentine wasn't as efficient. His mouth was tipping up humorously and a peculiar choking noise was coming from his throat. Moira blanched. The apple wasn't supposed to bite back.

She recovered instantly to probe: "But you haven't said whether you're going to enter?"

Sharon wondered if she could primly decline without losing face.

"The winner gets a blue sash to wear, a silver cup to keep for a year, and a cheque for twenty pounds. I'm told working girls are always notoriously hard up. Aren't you just a *tiny* bit tempted?"

Sharon was tempted. How she was

tempted! But not to join the six girls standing in a giggling, irresolute line by the platform.

"I don't think so," she began.

"Go on," urged Valentine. "Not many takers. Unless a few more join the ranks it isn't going to be much of a competition."

The attractive blonde headed the queue. Sharon thought it wasn't going to be much of a competition anyway. She looked at Tony, but he was looking in the opposite direction and really she didn't think he could save her, not with the odds so heavily fixed against. She didn't know how it had come about, but she couldn't refuse and cling to the image of being a good sport. All the same, she hated having to tag on to the end of the line. Tony might have flashed her a smile of encouragement, but he was looking anywhere but at her and so she was denied this solace. It wasn't as if she could win. Moira *wouldn't* give her her vote. Valentine *couldn't*. He'd urged her to join but he wouldn't feel able to vote for her. Under the spotlight he would have to be scrupulously fair and he would reason it out that living in the same house would give her an unfair bias. She might get Tony's vote. One never knew what to expect in that quarter.

The lead guitarist swung into one of those *pretty girl* ballads, so popular at such events, and the pianist came in with a quiver of tremolos. Sharon was acutely conscious of all the staring eyes. She tried to remember everything she had learned about deportment. Shoulders back, rib-cage high, buttock in, breathe naturally. How on earth did one breathe naturally?

Respite time. The judges voted. Each one cast a different vote because three finalists were called back. Because of the small number competing they hadn't intended to have an eliminating round. The three were, the blonde, a pretty dark girl in a slim fitting sheath of spicy cinnamon, and Sharon.

'Bless you,' she thought looking at

Tony. 'You did give me your vote.'

But what now? The judges had made judgement and didn't want to be swerved from their original choice. The Master of Ceremonies was asked to cast his vote, and the dilemma was settled. The blonde won.

Valentine did the honours. He slid the winner's blue sash over her head, handed her the cheque and the silver cup and, to the delight of the crowd, led her into the winner's waltz.

As Sharon watched, a hand took hold of her elbow, slid down her forearm and trapped her wrist. She didn't have to look to know it was Tony.

"Come on," he said.

It never occurred to her to ask where he was taking her. She followed slavishly. His bulk cleaved a way through the dancers, then he led her through an archway, down a wide echoing corridor and, after wrestling with a contraption of bolts, made her precede him through the door.

He closed it after them.

They were sharing a back yard with six dustbins, overlooked by the kitchen window. The blind of this was drawn down and it gave out only a narrow pencil-beam of light. There was no other illumination. Sharon thought there should be a moon, but she couldn't see one. She couldn't see anything. It was like going blind.

Tony was having the same difficulty.

"Where are you?" he said.

"Nowhere." She giggled. "I can't see it or feel it or touch it, so it must be nowhere."

Their eyes adjusted to the nothing-darkness and they saw again.

"Sorry I haven't provided a balcony and steps leading down into a floodlit garden," he said.

"Unrealistic props," she scoffed. "Who needs them anyway." She had been going to ask him why he had brought her here, but decided that could be categorised as a foolish question. His hands came down lightly

179

on her shoulders and after various innocent meanderings, settled around her waist. He talked pretty nonsense into her ear and the air was suddenly too potent to inhale so that it hurt just to breathe. His chin rubbed against her cheek and she felt the bristly imperfection of man; it was chafing and comforting and absurdly exhilarating.

She felt beautiful and cherished and warm and relaxed. She thought this is how an abandoned female must feel and she didn't care. And then he kissed her. Once, twice, three times. An orgy of kisses.

"Wow!" It felt like her but it sounded like him.

"What does that mean?"

"It means you're a very disturbing girl."

"I don't feel like a girl. I feel like a woman."

"That's what I mean. We should go back."

"Why?"

"Because I'm hungry."

"That's a brutal thing to say."

"No, it's not. If you think about it, it's a kind thing to say."

They went back through the door. She waited for him while he bolted all the bolts, and then together they walked back down the corridor.

"The refreshment room is that way," she said. "I glanced in earlier and got a preview of the goodies."

"Not yet. This way first."

"But you said you were hungry."

"And so I am. But it so happens that I'm already committed to have supper with someone. Oh, it's all right," he said, displaying a man-sized lack of tact, "she won't mind your joining us."

"Yes, but I might mind joining you." Her indignation gathered. "Tony, you can't mix your women as you'd mix your drinks. Go to her, if that's what you want." She called herself a woman, but because no one can transgress in a moment she sounded like a sulky little girl.

He gave her hand a tender tug. "Don't be a daft carrot. It's not that sort of a her."

He plunged her through a sickly sweet smelling, specially imported for the event, indoor garden. Exotic purple flowers, looking like plastic and feeling like velvet, grew alongside giant daffodils of greenhouse perfection, and trailing greenery brushed her bare arms and the concentrated scent of it all tingled her nose. Lovers' seats were set here and there at discreetly spaced intervals, and they passed those which were occupied with carefully, *tactfully* averted eyes until they arrived at a row of Bentwood chairs, sentinel straight and looking curiously out of place in this unrealistic setting. They overlooked a fountain with a stone parapet and dazzling aquamarine water.

Tony's supper date, a patiently waiting woman in a patiently waiting condition, sat on the second Bentwood chair from the end. Her hair was dark and cut short, she didn't have a very high forehead and her eyebrows were completely lost under her ragged fringe, making her eyes look enormous. They were puppy-dog brown and had that same wet-velvet sympathetic look about them, and were etched with a fine network of lines which spell out the late thirties or early forties. Her dress was bright yellow and it fanned out around her like the trumpet of one of those unbelievably huge daffodils. Betty Mason wasn't the only pregnant woman there and it didn't have to be her, but Sharon knew that it was. It was.

Was it her imagination, or did Tony cast her a special speculative look as he performed the introduction?

"Betty I've brought a friend to see you. Sharon — Betty."

"Hello."

"Hello."

"Are you not dancing?"

"Thanks for the compliment, love." She lowered her head and her fringe shook. "Actually, I'm waiting for the Elephant Tango."

"Really!" said Tony dryly. "I thought you were just here for the food."

"Don't remind me," she said, clutching her ample front. "I snack all the time. Eddie, that's my husband," she said nodding to Sharon, "says I have one meal a day. And that's how long it lasts, one day. I've a feeling that I shall pay the price and that even when I've ejected junior I shall still be lumping round this great roll of fat. The trouble is I'm always so hungry. Right now I could eat a horse."

"I'll go and see what I can find," obliged Tony. "What about you, Sharon. Any particular preference?"

"Will you think me terribly greedy if I say a bit of everything?" She confessed: "I'm famished."

"Is that so," said Betty, and Sharon had the feeling that her eyebrows were going up higher under cover of her fringe. "Do you mean to say you can *eat* in that dress?"

"I don't know. I haven't tried."

"You're being a trifle optimistic, I

should think. Your zip's wriggling down a bit at the back. Did you know?"

"No."

"The hook and eye isn't fastened at the top."

Tony stepped up with a gallant: "Permit me." She wondered what his reaction would be if he knew that was the second time she'd been zipped up in one evening. Certainly not a favourable one in view of the fact that his uncle had first performed the service.

"Oh that dress," Betty was saying enviously. "Or rather what's in it. Of course I couldn't possibly achieve your figure. I mean, I never had it to start with and you can't hope for what you've never had. But it would be nice to be lighter." Tony broke her sigh to say:

"I'll see what I can rustle up in the way of food."

"While you're gone I shall pump her," threatened Betty mischievously. "I like to know what's going on."

"That's all right," said Tony darkly. "She never tells."

Gone was the humour that had attractively lit up his eyes. As he looked straight at her, Sharon experienced a curious prickly feeling; she wanted to call back the fun-talk and defer permanently this serious turn. *She never tells*. He sounded bitter, ominous, as if he knew. Knew about that day which would never fade and grew more impregnable in her mind. The better she knew Tony, the more intolerable her burden. Her heart was heavy as she watched him walk away. She thought sadly that it wouldn't always be a quest for food. One day he might walk away for good.

"You and Tony," said Betty manoeuvring her thoughts away from a possibility too dreadful to contemplate. "Have you anything going?"

It was cheek, inquisitive cheek, and yet coming from nice Betty Mason it was impossible to take offence.

"The usual," replied Sharon honestly.

"It's not serious. He's amusing himself with me. And he's beastly to me. He hasn't danced with me yet and he calls me a daft carrot."

"That is beastly," said Betty with mock gravity. "My Eddie used to call me a scatty ha'porth. And the ha'penny isn't even currency any more. That dates me. You know, men never are serious. Take me and Eddie, we had a strictly no-strings friendship."

"What happened?"

The brown puppy-dog eyes glazed over sorrowfully.

"Patricia did."

"Oh, I am sorry."

"Why?" challenged Betty her chin going up. "We weren't the first. We won't be the last."

"That wasn't what I meant. I'm sorry for reminding you of Patricia. I tried to avoid mention of her, but now that I have, have you heard anything?"

"No."

"How dreadful for you. I don't know what to say."

"There's nothing you can say. I'm a failed mother, and that's all there is to it." She badly needed comfort; what comfort could Sharon give.

"Please don't say that. It isn't true."

"She went off on her own. That's true."

She found herself leaping to tackle that one.

"Do you think she did?"

Betty's eyes pierced hers, curiously intent. She realised the trap she was walking into. The horrible alternative she was suggesting.

"You are absolutely right. There isn't anything else to think. I suppose there comes a time in every girl's life when she has to assert her independence."

"Did you?"

"No."

"Nor I. I sometimes think I'm still fastened to my mother's apron strings, and I'm thirty-nine. Poor Pattie, poor little kid. How could I have been a proper mother to her when I've never taken the trouble to assert myself. Mine is the passive nature. I take what comes and hope it's palatable. Pattie isn't like me. I'll never forget the look on her face when I told her I was going to have a baby. She went as white as if she'd come from the dentist's."

"She didn't welcome the baby, then?"

"No. I don't much blame her for that because I didn't either at first. We erred by default, if you know what I mean. I could have been pregnant when Patricia was a toddler or anytime in between, but I had to wait until she was fifteen and me thirty-nine. It's no fun, you know, going to the ante-natal clinic. Nobody there looks a day over eighteen and I feel positively ancient."

"But you're happy now, aren't you?" probed Sharon with kindly interest. "You said you hated it at first, so that means you've come round to the idea of having a baby."

"Oh, sure. I'd like to give Eddie a boy. He'd like that. Every man craves a son. There I go, thinking it's mine to give. You think because your body houses them and feeds them and because you suffer all sorts of indignities to give them life, that they're yours. Then when they're fifteen they can take it into their head to run away and you discover they're not yours at all and probably never have been."

"Don't," said Sharon as the brown eyes filled up and the huge, daffodil trumpet dress began to quiver in a most alarming fashion. "Please don't upset yourself. It can't be good for you."

"I shouldn't have come. I didn't want to but Eddie said if I stayed at home I would only mope. Wonder where Tony is with the food. Funny, but I don't feel hungry any more. I . . . feel . . . "

"Are you all right?"

"Shall be in a tick," she said, the moment she could summon up sufficient breath, which considerably increased Sharon's mounting concern.

"I just got a . . . ooh . . . there it is again. Not a pain exactly, more of a . . . ooh!" Her face contorted and her hands twisted, more in anger than anguish, as if she couldn't fathom her own stupidity. "I *was* right. I shouldn't have come. Look, love, I don't want to alarm you, but do you think you can find my husband for me? Be as quick as you can," she said, closing her eyes as her body gave another violent wrench.

Sharon didn't say a word. She just ran. She'd often wondered how she'd fare if it ever fell upon her to deliver a message of terrific importance against odds of time. She'd imagined that urgency would give her the essential speed and that without any self-effort she'd gain a pair of silver heels and a miraculously clear brain.

It wasn't true. Her legs felt like useless lumps of dough and had to be pushed and pummelled into every step. And she was in the ballroom and peering anxiously at faces before it dawned on her that she didn't know Edward Mason from Adam. He might be the short, tubby man propping up the entrance, or the man with the balding topknot, somewhat like a monk's tonsure, dancing with the girl in green.

Tony. Tony would know. The refreshment room. She turned. And cannoned into Valentine.

"Betty Mason," she gasped.

"I see." It couldn't have been what she said, so it must have been how she looked. "Get your breath back," he insisted. "A few seconds can't matter." Then he did something rather sweet. He took her face in his hands and held it there for a moment until she collected herself. She had always thought that was an essentially stupid saying. But then, she'd never before fallen apart and had to pick up all the little bits of herself and fit them together until everything co-ordinated and she could truthfully say: "I'm all right now. Please help me. How can I find Edward Mason?"

"Ask for him by name at the refreshment counter. I'll try the bar."

She didn't get as far as the refreshment room. She didn't need to. She spotted Tony and Detective Sergeant Thompson, the policeman who'd called at the house about Patricia Mason, in deep conversation with a third man. The third man was Edward Mason. She didn't have to be told this. She knew. She took one look at the grave expressions on their faces, and her heart went cold.

11

TONY was the first to sense her presence. He swung sharply round to see her standing in the doorway, her face was white, save for the smattering of freckles on her nose. Her eye contained a wild unfathomable look. She said hoarsely:

"Bad news?" Her fingertips locked together, in an attitude of prayer.

He spoke gently, ruled by a surprisingly compassionate lump that rose to his throat.

"I'm sorry, Sharon, but it's not good. Edward has to go with the detective sergeant. Question of identifying a body. Don't tell Betty. No point in alarming her. And it might not be Patricia. Will you go back to Betty. Stay with her." She looked stunned. He wondered if she properly understood. He said:

"You're not going to be much of a comfort unless you can — "

She got the drift and didn't allow him to finish. "It's all right. I'll cover up. It's just that there is a slight complication. I think, that is *Betty thinks* she's starting the baby." Automatically she had addressed Edward Mason. She saw a look of gentle agony possess his face and said impulsively:

"Don't worry about this end. Tony and I will take Betty to the hospital. You go with the detective sergeant." She touched his arm. "I hope the news isn't bad."

Between them they managed to fob Betty off with something about Edward having to go to the police station because of a possible lead. She seemed satisfied with the explanation. Perhaps she was in no condition to reason that it would have to be something sickeningly important for him to desert her at that crucial moment. That, or perhaps she was being terribly brave. Or just plain sensible because to give way, to indulge in even a mild fit of hysterics could not improve the macabre turn of events.

Because of Tony's nimble driving skill coupled with incredible good luck at the traffic lights, they reached the hospital in record time. Betty looked horrible. All eyes and anxiety and she admitted grimly that Patricia hadn't been in *this* much of a hurry and she'd half expected the baby to be born in the car.

With shared relief, they handed her over to a slip of a nurse who, despite her youth, seemed to know all about that sort of thing, and collapsed thankfully on waiting-room chairs.

"I didn't think we were going to make it," said Sharon in a suspiciously thin voice. He shot a keen appraising look.

"You've been wonderful," he praised. "Don't you dare black out on me now." His hand felt warm and firm on top of hers. Her attack of giddiness receded, the distempered walls stopped looking like floating panels of silk and again looked like distempered walls, and his voice stopped coming and going, like a faulty sound recording.

"I'll fetch you some tea. As soon as you're safe to leave."

"I'm safe."

"Sure? I don't want you keeling over."

"Positive. I'd love some tea. Will there be any?"

"I don't know. I might have to charm one of the nurses."

You'll do it beautifully, she thought as she watched him walk away.

He came back in an indecently short time — she hoped he hadn't appropriated someone else's life-saving brew, because there hadn't been time to make any — carrying a metal tray on which sat two cups of tea. Each saucer contained one arrowroot biscuit and one lump of sugar.

"Sister?"

"Matron, no less."

"Nice."

"Delectable, if you mean the matron. I don't know about the tea. Don't you want your sugar?"

"I don't take it."

"May I?"

"Of course."

She watched him transfer the lump of sugar from her saucer and drop it into his cup. He stirred vigorously.

"What would have happened if — ?"

She closed her eyes. "I daren't think about it. But what's your worry? *You* were driving. What went on in the back was definitely my province. I was," — she slid him a mischievous look — "sorry, I can't resist it — holding the baby."

"Almost," he corrected.

"Yes," she agreed with heartfelt relief.

Both were aware of deliberately driving away from mention of Edward's unhappy mission. The driving force, the talk, ran out. Sharon studied the bubbles on her tea, watched the last one pop and disappear. She sought for something to latch on to, a ballast, a thought, to relieve the active waiting.

There's a time for action and a time for waiting. Sometimes the waiting is as active as the action, when the mind grinds on after the legs have stopped.

The events of the evening had unnerved her more than a little. They'd come whirling at her, one after the other, without respite, until her senses had reached swimming pitch and her head was a jumble of chaotic thoughts. To begin with, she couldn't help feeling that Valentine's unexpected proposal was without precedent. She'd heard enough gossip to know that her sex found him wickedly attractive and that he used their interest shamelessly. He was the perfect parallel of the married man enjoying his status because of the freedom it gave him. 'But, my love, you *knew* I was married.'

She felt deeply touched that he hadn't used that line on her, that he regarded her as someone above a scurrilous affair. It was nice to be set apart, thought of as different. A far cry from Tony's cavalier treatment. She was a fool to respond to his kisses the way she did. It gave him a tactical advantage. A girl shouldn't willingly give up every little bit of herself. She felt certain it was a sign of naïvety to be so lacking in subtlety and wisdom. She wished her experience was less limited and then perhaps it wouldn't be such an uphill struggle just to cope. He'd made a moderately passionate pass. She remembered the other time and amended that to two moderately passionate passes. So what! Wouldn't she have felt anxious if he had shown no desire to want to kiss and pet her. But if only it were just that, if only he didn't use her as a landing base for hurtful sarcastic remarks. She wondered which he enjoyed the most, petting her or taunting her with his sharp tongue. It wouldn't be so bad if he'd change the record now and again. Always it was the same theme. The lady never tells. It was an obsession with him. This evening when Betty, indulging in a spot of innocent fun, had threatened to pump her, he'd treated it as something dark and sinister. And those remarks he'd made that other evening about her being like the rest of them and willing to pay her corner. If only his disapproval wasn't so enduring. It would help to know what it was he so strongly disapproved of.

She chanced a quick glance at him. His face was as hospital-blighted as her own. This place, the waiting, would give anybody the jitters, but these weren't normal hospital jitters. Why didn't the nurse come with some news? Why didn't Edward come? Poor Edward — she couldn't resist the thought one moment longer — he must be going through an impossibly harrowing experience.

Life and death. How often they are uttered in the same breath. It's a matter of life and death. Such a well-worn expression, as if one is reliant on the other. Is it like that? *Is* life a matter of death? They say that before a child can be born, someone, somewhere, has to die. If no one died the world would be an impossible place to live in. And yet, and yet . . .

She was conscious of the unnaturally loud tick of the wall clock — the door opening — the feeling that this was the beginning of the end of the waiting period.

It was Edward and the nice detective sergeant. One look at their faces, just *one* look and they knew. The tick of the clock subsided and natural noises — breathing — could be heard again.

The detective sergeant sent Sharon a brilliantly warm smile of recognition. Edward said simply:

"It wasn't Patricia."

At three minutes past midnight Betty gave birth to a son.

Sharon was glad it wasn't Patricia who had to die to give him the chance of life.

"Poor Sharon," sympathised Tony. "You didn't get your supper."

"No," she said without regret.

"You look exhausted and yet, in a strange way, exhilarated. You are a contradictory creature, did you know?"

"No," she said sleepily, happily, from her side of the car. It was, for the most part, a silent drive as they were both in a reactive stupor after the hectic events of the evening. At times they had been physically closer, and yet they'd never been as near to one another as they were then, bowling down the empty roads under a sky the colour of faded ebony, no visible moon and only a light sequin of stars.

Part way he stopped the car and gathered her to him with a surprisingly tender touch. It was a ghost embrace, unmarred by passion and desire, giving not taking. Perhaps that was the moment to tell her secret, but right then she couldn't have found a single word. Silently, wonderingly, she accepted this unexpected gift of comfort and revelled in being cared for. In accepting she felt her heart swell with joy and she forgot all manner of things. Lack of trust. That she was vulnerable, capable of being hurt. The fear that he would one day walk away, the loneliness that would be lonelier for having known him.

A blunt finger teased the tip of her chin. "Not the Belle of the Ball but — " He started the car and the last two words were drowned by the roar of the engine, but she thought he said 'You'll do.'

They were seated at the kitchen table with the companionable remains of a meal between them when Moira and Valentine came home.

Sharon automatically braced herself, then forgot everything in her compassion for Valentine. His face was a white mask with ragged black holes torn out for eyes and a tightly compressed line for a mouth.

'Fatigue,' was the doctor's verdict when he called the next day. Nothing a few day's rest wouldn't cure, but nevertheless a warning that he still had to take things steady unless he was prepared to pay the price.

That's why she didn't panic as much as she normally would have done at losing the earrings. The loss seemed trivial after seeing that look of death on Valentine's face.

Because of everything, she didn't miss them until next morning. She looked at the scatter of hairpins on her dressing-table and expected the earrings to be with them. They weren't there. She tried to remember taking them off, but it was difficult. Removing clothing, taking out hairpins, removing earrings, brushing hair: all automatic gestures that one rarely remembers with certainty. But she didn't think she'd removed the earrings because for her that wouldn't have been automatic. She rarely, if ever, wore jewellery. Besides which, they were so pretty she didn't think she could have taken them off without holding them in her hand for a moment, admiring them. She must have lost them some time during the evening.

Without hope, she telephoned the

place where the dance had been held and enquired if a pair of earrings had been handed in.

"A pair? That's unusual,"

"What is?"

"Well, it's *usually* one. Not that it makes any difference. None have been handed in."

"Oh."

"Look, if you care to give me your name and address and a description of the earrings, I'll get in touch if they do turn up."

Sharon complied, omitting the important detail that the stones were real. Girls in her position didn't own real diamonds. If she'd considered this embarrassing possibility she wouldn't have let Valentine talk her into borrowing them. Why had she? Not because she coveted them, pretty as they were, but because she had found it too difficult to refuse. He'd been such a hurt little boy and he had taken such a lot of pleasure at the thought of her wearing them.

"What do you reckon the chances are of their turning up?"

"Slight," she was informed.

She politely murmured her thanks, trying not to sound too dispirited, and rang off.

Patricia Mason came back the day after the dance. Sharon supposed she must have explained her disappearance to the satisfaction of her parents and presumably, as they had been called in, the police. She heard the several circulating rumours. The most credible was that Patricia had gone to stay with an out-of-touch relative. It was said she hadn't troubled to inform anyone because she didn't think anyone cared. Credible, pathetic.

As soon as Valentine was sufficiently recovered, she sought him out to tell him about losing the earrings. They say confession is good for the soul. That may be, but it doesn't do much for the knees. When he told her to sit down she did so thankfully, pressing her hands together to stop them from shaking. Her voice had to make out the best it could.

"The earrings," she began badly. "I," she faltered. Then stopped.

His mouth moved into a smile.

"I know," he helped out.

"You know?" Hope, warm and instantaneous coloured her tone.

"Obviously you've changed your mind. You want to keep them. That's it, isn't it? My dear, it's only what I expected and I should be delighted — "

"No, Valentine," she cut in brusquely. "That's not it. For a moment I thought — " She looked down at her hands, then back up at him. "I don't know what I thought. The truth is I want to give them back. But I can't. I've lost them."

"You've lost them?" he repeated. He shook his head, finding it impossible to believe and she felt chilled by the perplexity and penetration of his gaze. "I don't understand. The fasteners were adequate."

"I don't understand *either*. I don't

see how I *could* have lost them, but I have." Her voice was high, her fingers tensely interlaced, and there was a snapping tightness about her mouth.

He studied her for a lightning summing up moment, then cast aside his own justifiable annoyance to say lightly:

"Steady. They were only a pair of earrings."

It wasn't at all what she expected.

"Only?" A brightness of tears gathered in her eyes. "Please don't be so kind. They were beautiful and valuable." His hand clamped down on her shoulder.

"You're getting into a state and all for nothing. Nothing," he repeated as she would have protested. "Look, you say the earrings are valuable. At one time I might have agreed with you, but values are relative. Mine have changed over the past months. Now I value waking up each morning. I value the feel of the sun on the back of my hand, the rain splashing on my face. Silly things, such as walking along and hearing the wind and imagining it's saying my name. Ever played that game?" He didn't give her time to answer — he frequently phrased questions but rarely waited for answers — "Of course you have," he claimed decisively. "With a name like yours you *must* have." He spoke her name and his breath soughed against her cheek. "And sunsets, Sharon. You can't know what a lift I get to see a truly splendid sunset. Ah! now you are smiling and I can confess my greatest thrill, which is to see a smile on your face. You can't know, you can't even begin to imagine, what happiness that gives me. So let's have no more unhappy looks. Let's have a drink and forget all about those silly earrings." His voice was warm and coaxing, then full of concern as he noted her pallor. Distress had stolen the glow from her cheeks. "What is it?" he demanded with the kindliest of intent. "Why do you look so peculiar?"

"I'm stunned. I didn't think anyone

could be so — kind. I'll have a drink with you, but tea. And I'll fetch it in a little while. First," — she swallowed — "will it be dreadfully embarrassing?"

"Will what?" His eyes were blank.

"The formalities. You know, filling in all those beastly insurance forms."

"No." His finger abstractedly drew patterns. "It won't be embarrassing at all." He side-stepped: "Tea, isn't it too late in the day for tea?"

"Not for me and it's better for you than whisky." She refused to bite on that so patently obvious red herring and said: "Why won't it be embarrassing?"

He shifted his glance. "You are far too persistent for your own peace of mind," he warned. A remark which served to increase her determination. Troubled, she demanded:

"Valentine, you must tell me."

"Yes, I see I must. Well the fact is — " But her brain had stumbled on ahead and the fact came swinging at her.

"You haven't insured. Is that it?"

"I didn't want to tell you."

"But isn't that horribly negligent," she fatally said the first thing that came into her head.

His reply was mingled with grimness and amusement.

"Yes. That makes us quits, doesn't it? We've both been horribly negligent, as you put it. So now will you let the matter drop."

"How can I?" She was caught in a crossfire of thought. It was too shattering. All this kindness. His calm matter-of-fact acceptance. She said stiffly:

"You're right. It is too late in the day for tea. I will have something stronger. Would it be too pretentious of me to offer to pay? I suppose it would take a lifetime."

His mouth lifted into a sweet and gentle smile. Not a bit patronising, but the sort of carefree, joyous expression she would willingly have given her soul to the devil to achieve, except, she thought miserably, if she did give up

212

her soul she wouldn't have anything to be joyful about.

He was saying:

"Contrary to your imaginings they weren't all that expensive. So stop being so melodramatic. Stop it do you hear!"

"Yes, Valentine," said Sharon biting her lip. There wasn't anything else she could say. Except — because it was beginning to be a bit of an obsession with her — "You are very kind. I've never met anyone as kind."

12

SHE wanted to run away from Swallow Heights again. The day was fast rolling to a close. The sun had been taken in and the flowers were all tucked up in their beds; it was the hour of dusk, of enchantment. She didn't know what it was she wanted to run away from.

Tony rescued her. His car blazed a trail of light up the winding tree-whipped drive and she watched from the drawing-room window. Watched, hoped, waited. She didn't know that Tony was going to rescue her. Neither did Tony.

He thought it was an impulse. All his own idea. He entered the room and there she was. The flame of her hair lit the curve of her neck and her childishly light perfume evaded definition. He took a step forward and then he didn't want to define her perfume any more. He wanted to kiss her. Instead his hand enclosed her elbow.

"Where are you taking me?"

"Out."

"Why?" It sounded neither provocative nor ingenuous.

"Ah!" he said.

"No."

"No?"

She danced out of his grasp — almost reached the door.

"Not until I've changed."

She left her day dress at home but she took her nerves, her jumpiness, with her. She had to hold her breath as the car rushed through the wide double gates, took the bend with a raw squeal of tyres, and sped recklessly down the curving snake of road.

"You take the corners too fast," she said.

"Do I?" His eyes lazily and frighteningly crept round to hers.

"Either reduce speed or keep your eyes front."

"Relax. I know this road as well as I know the back of my hand."

"That's all very well. But what if we meet someone coming the other way?"

"This is a private road," he reminded. "Who'd be coming?"

"Visitors," she suggested.

"Yes," he admitted. "A possibility. Although, there hasn't been many since dear Valentine's illness."

"Why do you call your uncle, dear Valentine in that derogatory fashion? Don't you like him?"

"Of course I like him." She would have taken the words at their face value but for the fact that his voice was thick with sarcasm and implied a contradictory meaning. "Haven't you noticed how likeable he is? Of course you must have," he said, following his uncle's trick of not waiting for an answer. "He never wastes time getting to work on people to make them like him. There's some cigarettes in the glove compartment."

216

"I don't smoke."

"No, but I do. Light one for me."

She did. Her mouth closed on the filter tip and as the end glowed like a jewel in the failing light, the strong, unpleasant taste of tobacco made her grimace and she wondered that people found pleasure in smoking. She wondered at a lot of exhilarating, sensuous things that pass for pleasure. It gave her pleasure to think of him quietly smoking the cigarette she had lit for him, his lips touching where hers had touched. In passing it over their fingers brushed, increasing the sense of intimacy. Perhaps it was because she had never lit a man's cigarette before, but she was filled with a warm-shivery feeling, a feeling that could not altogether be disassociated with his nearness and the pale misty magic of the night.

Magic. She'd been out with other boys and they'd made happy times together. But Tony was different, dangerously different, because just by being together, without props or artifice, they made magic.

Boys — and that was another thought that pulled her up with a jerk. Tony had transgressed and was no longer a boy but had entered the league of men. Beside him she felt very much in the junior class and she wondered if she could cope. It was a miracle that he wanted to date her. Could she continue to hold his interest or in time would she bore him silly with her girlish chatter. Except that she wasn't talking much now. His nearness seemed to evoke a curious dryness that paralysed her vocal chords and almost closed her throat.

"Refreshing," he said.

"What is?"

"A girl in a quiet, pensive mood. Or are you deliberating on whether or not you find my uncle likeable. I said you would, now I come to think about it *you* didn't say anything."

"No, I didn't. Yes I find him likeable. No I don't find him likeable."

"You still haven't said anything."

"I can't. He both attracts and repels me, if you know what I mean. I don't want to like him. I think that liking him will in some way harm me, though I'm blessed if I know how. Yet I can't help myself. As you say, he works at it and by sheer — I almost said brute force, but there's nothing brutal about him. So charm, the charm of a little boy, which is infinitely more potent because it's harder to resist. It's the silent appeal in his eyes that does the trick. And of course he is so kind." Her lips parted to let escape an involuntary sigh. "He's so incredibly kind."

Tony reacted to her final words by jerking his head and frowning hard at the road ahead, the very set of his neck showing his displeasure. But Sharon didn't notice. Then he said:

"While you're being honest, were you thinking about him while you were in that deep thinking silence?"

Sharon, remembering her thoughts, repressed a laugh and truthfully said:

"No."

Although his shoulders relaxed against the back of the seat, his voice was brusque. "You've a very teasing way with you. Most women wouldn't have been able to resist elaborating a little."

She was conscious of two things. That he was a difficult man to understand. And that the lovely benign mood could easily slip from her grasp.

Funny, but she set up a similar reaction in him, as Valentine did in her. He liked her because he couldn't help it. He was attracted in spite of himself by — what? Though her bedroom boasted two mirrors she was modest enough to be bemused by this question. Anyway, the mirror girls were more often seen sideways or walking away. Frontways they were always too busily occupied combing hair or putting on lipstick to actually pause and do nothing but look.

"You're a very beautiful girl," he said thoughtfully. "But I suppose you've been told that before."

"That sort of repetition I don't mind

220

in the least," she said with a laugh. Unexpectedly he asked:

"What were you like when you were four?"

She pondered. "Difficult question that. I hadn't known myself long enough to form an opinion. You tell me."

"All right. You had match-stick legs and orange hair and your toes turned in and nobody could have guessed that you'd turn out to be such a little belter."

"You know, you've only just redeemed yourself. Actually, I was a very attractive child. You're dead right about the toes turning in, though. I used to trip over them and fall flat on my nose. I was ten before anyone realised I had freckles because they were permanently concealed under a brown scab."

"I should like to have known you at ten."

"Would you? I doubt it. You'd be what — eighteen? I *very* much doubt it."

They both laughed.

Incautiously she admitted: "I'd like to have known you at eighteen when you were all gorgeous charm and magnetism and before you — " She needn't have stopped. Their thoughts had run a collision course and met head-on.

"Go on," he urged, "say it. Or shall I say it for you? Before I grew bitter and cynical."

"I'm sorry." Sorry she'd clumsily dropped the meringue-light conversation and watched its sweetness ooze away. And, as everyone knows, a dropped meringue cannot be reclaimed. At best it can be mopped up — and nothing.

His square hands tightened on the wheel. She sat next to him and yet she might have been a million miles away. He isolated her with one sharp sentence. "What's a nice girl like you doing in a set-up like this?"

She could have asked what set-up. She could have said take me to the moon. She would have got the same response. She said:

"If it's going to be like this, we might as well turn back." She put her fingers up to her neck, twisting it slightly to ease a tautness. The moon floated into being above a wooded slope and the road rolled away and the car bit into the tarmac, chasing it with renewed determination.

"Never turn back, Sharon. Always press forward. It's all right. It's not altogether you. And I want us to be friends."

So did she. *So did she.*

"Where are we going?" she asked after a while.

"To the Flying Fox. They do a good meal."

She hurried to meet the friendliness in his tone. The meringue's spilled so let's have jam.

"Lovely."

"Hungry?"

"Famished."

The tension eased. As they walked across the pub's forecourt he caught hold of her hand, giving it a gentle squeeze. It was his way of saying thank you for bearing with me. To get to the dining-room they had to squash a way through the main bar. The tables were full, so they squashed back. She waited while he filched two stools from under the nose of an individual with less of everything: determination, sheer charming impudence — so that's how it was done! — and then they sat up at the bar on the acquired stools and sipped sherry and ate salted nuts and potato crisps until a beckoning waiter indicated it was their turn for a table.

Sharon took one look at the large and impressive menu, and left the choice to Tony. It was obvious he'd been before and, as he predicted the cuisine was good. When Sharon said she was famished that wasn't quite the truth, but when the food was placed in front of her her appetite perked up and she was able to lay her knife and fork down on an empty plate.

"That was delicious."

The waiter whisked away their plates

and brought dishes of fresh fruit salad topped with cream. Tony watched, amused, as she appreciatively dug in her spoon. He said:

"Shari would have met her match in you. My sister was the only other girl I took out who did justice to her food. She used to say the reason she ate so well was because she had nothing on her conscience."

If he'd said 'Oh, by the way, I've planted a bomb under your chair' the result couldn't have been more unexpected. Every bit of colour drained from her face, leaving it parchment, except for the freckles on her nose which stood out like luminous golden blobs. Her fingernails scraped the tablecloth to disappear in a tight little ball on her lap, and her lips clamped together, terrified of indiscreetly spilling something they shouldn't. He threw down his spoon and said:

"This is getting to be quite ridiculous. You will tell me, even if I have to beat it out of you." Yet he spoke so coolly, so rationally, his mouth fixed in that same little smile that she wondered if she'd heard right.

"You're being deliberately provocative again," he accused. "Anybody would think you were holding out for diamonds."

She stared at him, agonised, and then began to shake with helpless laughter. "Not diamonds. I'm not fit for diamonds. I lose them."

"You what?"

"Lose them," she repeated to effect.

"If you're trying to change the subject," he said, "you've succeeded. We'll let the other ride for a moment. You'd better tell me about the diamonds. Where and when did you lose them?"

She answered, not caring that he was humouring her:

"At the staff dance. The property of your uncle." His interest crisped; she could almost hear it clicking into attentiveness. "Earrings. A loan, you understand." She sounded so priggishly, beautifully serious he dare not laugh.

"I'll try to," he said. It was a failed attempt because she uttered a small scandalised gasp and declared:

"I did lose a pair of valuable earrings."

"I'm sure you did," he affirmed. "And when you confessed the loss *dear* Valentine was shocked. But he covered up remarkably well, and he was so incredibly kind — your words I believe — and you are now indebted to him for life."

"Yes," she drew back from him — "but you're making it sound horrible. You're making him sound a monster and he was sweet, and yes!" — her chin lifted defiantly — "kind."

"Of course. It's his stock in trade. We've already established that he works at it."

"Yes but — "

"But me no buts. Listen. Did you want to wear the earrings?"

"No."

"How did he tempt you?"

She was forced to admit: "He didn't. He just went on and on until I couldn't refuse."

"That figures. You've no idea when you lost them?"

"None."

"You didn't take them off because they nipped?"

"No. Because they didn't. They were so comfy I didn't know I was wearing them. Why do you ask?"

"Because you were wearing them for the Belle of the Ball competition. I noticed them when you were in the line-up. Afterwards, at the hospital, I saw you weren't wearing them. Did you, by any chance, get into a clinch with anyone in between?"

"Yes." Colour flooded her cheeks. "You."

He smiled. "Well I didn't take them." His smile turned into delight.

"I'm pretty darned certain you were wearing them then. Lethal things." He rubbed the side of his face. "Wonder

I'm not maimed for life. But seriously, think."

"I am thinking. No one touched me apart from you."

His mouth softened. "Really? I like the sound of that. No one?" He leaned forward and took her face in his hands and held it there for a moment. She stiffened. Because that's what Valentine had done, put his hands up to her face and held it.

He stopped playing with the lobe of her ear and was just beginning to look hurt when she said:

"It's not you, Tony."

"Oh? Then why did you suddenly freeze up? Nobody's looking. Not more than six."

"Six. Six hundred. I don't care. I've just remembered that Valentine did that. Put his hands up to my face. It was when Betty started with the baby and I came tearing out to find you. He made me stop to get my breath back."

"And obviously swiped the earrings,"

229

Tony finished for her.

"Yes, but why? It doesn't make sense. I didn't want them for keeps."

"Did you tell him so?"

"Of course I did," she said rashly, running headlong into the trap he'd set.

"So he did offer them as a gift."

"Yes," she grudgingly admitted.

"Well! I'm glad you're above diamonds."

"No woman is above diamonds," she said daringly. "If it's the right man."

"M'mmm." Intently he studied her face. "There's an intriguing possibility there that must be deferred. Meanwhile — "

"Meanwhile, we're left puzzling as to why he should steal his own property."

"No we're not. That's obvious."

"Not to me it isn't."

"Perhaps it wouldn't be to me," he admitted generously, "if I didn't know how his mind works. People are easier to manipulate if he has something on them."

"Manipulate?"

"Use, then."

"I still don't see."

"Well, I could be wrong. But I think he's using you to keep me. At the moment, obviously, I'm something of an asset to him. While you're around I'm going to be reasonably content."

"You dislike your uncle very much. So why don't you leave?"

"I did once. After years of despising myself for letting him use me, I managed to make the break. I was doing very well, thank you very much, until this heart thing caught up with him. And down went the trap."

"He could hardly have staged that," she pointed out reasonably, "Anyway, he's better now. He can't need you as much."

"True enough. But now there's Jennifer to consider. I could take her with me, but what would a bachelor do with a twelve year old girl? Anyway, I'm curious."

"Curious?"

"I want to know what it's all about. And you won't tell me." His voice was reproachful.

"That's because I don't know."

His eyes met and held hers. "Is that the truth? I thought you were part of the intrigue. First Moira. Then you."

"Isn't Moira in love with you?"

"No. Moira's in love with Valentine."

"She doesn't act it."

"There are more ways than one of acting a part. Moira is what Valentine wants her to be. For some devious reason of his own, he wanted her to be nice to me. Dear Valentine doesn't care whom he sacrifices in his own best interest. If it was a sacrifice. Personally I think Moira's on borrowed time and while I feel desperately sorry for her, I don't fancy uncle's leavings."

"You never let it show," Sharon couldn't resist digging.

"I wouldn't be so ungallant," he teased.

"So when I turned up you thought I was a deliberate plant and that I'd been engaged to . . . to . . . But I think that's disgusting!"

"No." He rubbed his thumb down the side of his nose. "That part was rather nice."

"You horrible beast!" Her back straightened and her freckles stood out again.

"Guilty." The twinkle in his eye belied the abashed straightness of his mouth. "But I thought . . . well, I thought you'd come in with your eyes open and so it served you jolly well right. And then again, I was curious."

"Oh?"

"To find out how far you were willing to go to keep the lad content. Good grief!" Now his back shot up straight. "Why didn't you slap my face?"

The obliterating blush started in her cheeks and swept up to her hairline.

"I've asked that same question of myself. It must be because . . . because . . . "

233

Suddenly, the dining-room, with it's soft pink lighting and well spaced tables, seemed unbearably overcrowded.

★ ★ ★

Tony stopped the car at what she had come to think of as Jennifer's third bend.

"They'll see from the house," she protested.

"Nonsense. We're well screened by the trees. They can't see."

"That's what I mean. They'll have seen the car's headlights climbing the road and they'll know where we've stopped and why we've stopped. After what you've said I feel like a pawn in a game of chess. I want to make you happy because I want to make you happy. Not because he needs you for his rotten business. Where do you think he's put the earrings?"

"In his safe. Where else."

"Where is his safe?"

"In his bedroom. Appropriately

enough, behind the picture of a very luscious lady. But don't get any ideas."

"Why not. I could get into his bedroom."

"I don't doubt that for a moment." His voice thickened. "But just you try and I'll personally scalp you."

"But don't you see, if I found the earrings it would force the issue, whatever the issue is."

"I'll do the finding and the forcing. Keep that," — he lightly tweaked the tip of her nose — "out of it."

"But . . . but . . . "

"If you want to do something, do what you're being paid to do. Keep an eye on Jennifer."

She was suddenly alert. "Do you think that's necessary?"

He frowned. "I don't know. It was something that just came to me."

"Tony I th — "

"Stop thinking, stop being argumentative. Start being amenable."

She started to ask how, but his

mouth began to collect kisses and by
the time hers was free to speak it was
no longer a matter of pressing urgency
and could even be called a superfluous
question.

13

THE day came in slowly, rimming her bedroom with grey, then a thin grey-yellow before flooding it with a clear golden light. She woke in stages. The murky greyness sent her head sleepily back into her pillow, the thin grey-yellow was like a finger resting on her eyelids, the golden light penetrated beneath, easing them open.

Things settled, resolved, slid back as doubts. It was the day's fault. It brought with it, besides sunshine, further proof of Valentine's kindness, his understanding.

First he understood Jennifer. She'd got toothache and he handled her as though she was a piece of fragile glass. Anyone that sensitive to another's feelings couldn't be the villain Tony made out. Yesterday, with Tony, she'd accepted his summing up. Not only had it seemed feasible but the power of his certainty had been so strong and convincing that automatically she'd been pulled in. Today watching Valentine's finger touch Jennifer's flushed cheek, she found it easy to toss aside Tony's opinion. She didn't like Valentine any better, she still loved and hated him in the same breath of thought, and as intensely as before, but she couldn't think badly of him. He infuriated her as a child might infuriate her, and who could hold a grudge against a child? Next time she was with Tony she must tell him how wrong he was. Make him see that his uncle was really a little boy, with little boy sulks and mischief and demands, but with no real harm in him.

"Jennifer's got toothache," said Valentine. "She should be taken to the dentist's."

"Have you got toothache, Jennifer?"

"It's gone now." — hopefully.

"The tooth should be seen to," persisted Valentine. "Open your mouth.

There's a tiny piece broken off. See it?"

"M'm," said Sharon. "How did you do that, love?"

"I bit into a . . . into something hard." The child looked anguished, but then she would, wouldn't she?

Sharon spared her a brief sympathetic thought, then she was back to that day and she could hear again Shari's agitated voice. 'She bit into something and snapped off a tiny piece of tooth.'

"Gracious!" she exclaimed unthinkingly. "Hasn't that been seen to yet?"

"Yet?" Although Valentine spoke quietly it rumbled through her brain with all the warning intensity of a thunderbolt. "Jennifer has only just told me. Am I to understand you already knew? Did you tell anyone else, Jennifer? Anyone?"

"Yes." A pause. "I told Mummy."

Two pairs of eyes ranged against her. One troubled and accusative, the other — Valentine's — mildly perplexed.

239

"Then I couldn't possibly have known, could I?" said Sharon, struggling to right her slip.

"But you did, didn't you?" pressed Valentine later when Jennifer had gone to school and they were sharing a mid-morning pot of coffee. "Know Shari, I mean. It doesn't matter whether you knew about the tooth or not. Surely that's unimportant." He shrugged his shoulders to lighten his words, but his mouth thrust down at the corners, a perfect example of an obdurate small boy.

"I didn't know Shari," she was able to truthfully reply. He lifted a waggish finger. "Now you're splitting hairs. I don't mean know in the sense of know as a friend. But you were acquainted." His head tilted. "I think you have spoken with her on at least one occasion. Come now, admit that I'm right."

He was too persuasive; add that to a compelling desire to unburden. And:

"Just once. I spoke with her once

on the telephone." He didn't comment and his expectancy of waiting prodded her into further indiscretion.

"It was the day she died. I was alone in the office when she phoned. She was at a loose end and so I said why didn't she join me as I would be glad of the company, but — "

"She didn't make it," Valentine finished for her. "My dear, how agonising for you."

"It was *rather*." She searched for a non-existent handkerchief and gratefully accepted the one he offered. His handkerchief, then his shoulder.

"There, there," he soothed patting her head. "It will pass. The edge of your responsibility will blunt. Time is a great healer." He kept on muttering platitudes and in her overwrought state, because her guilt had weighed heavily, and it was such a relief to tell someone that it didn't occur to her that lavish as he was with the sympathy he was saying all the wrong words. He didn't say 'A human can't be held responsible for life' but accepted her guilt as a matter of course, so that instead of easing, her burden increased.

And yet, he was so incredibly gentle with her — and kind. Damn you Tony! Yes, kind, kind, *kind*!

"Better?"

"I think so." She didn't sound very sure, but he said: "Good." And, hooking his finger round a strand of her hair, gave it a playful tug.

"This weepy Sharon is a new one on me. I like her best with her chin up and smiling."

"Like this?"

"I like this very much," he said rewarding her attempt. "When Shari phoned, did she say anything?"

"She said about Jennifer's tooth."

"Nothing else?"

"She wanted to contact Tony."

"Oh?"

"She seemed het-up, anxious about something. She was very disappointed that he'd already left."

"She didn't make a confidant of you then?"

"No."

"I thought she might have had the urge to confide in someone and sometimes a stranger's ear is very tempting."

"She didn't tell me what it was that was upsetting her."

"Was she very upset?"

"Yes, I would say she was."

"M'm," He emerged from his thoughts to say: "I wouldn't mention it to Tony, if I were you. He and Shari were very close, you know, and he might feel bitter towards you. Of course, when you invited her round you didn't *know* you were going to be instrumental in her death, so you can't *really* be blamed. But Tony might not see it in the same way as you and I. Much better for you to say nothing."

"I'd made up my mind to that already. You don't think it's — "

"What?"

"Well, cowardly of me."

"No. I think you are a remarkably spirited girl. You must know what I think about you."

Dear Valentine. He couldn't be capable of the things Tony said. That must, surely, be an over-imaginative bit of reasoning.

She was still pondering and sighing when Valentine came back to tell her he'd phoned the dentist to make an appointment. It was fixed for four-thirty the following day.

Sharon felt fidgety for the rest of the day. She took this restless mood to bed with her. She thumped her pillow and turned it. She was too warm so she threw off the eiderdown. Then she felt too cold so she pulled it back up. She lay perfectly still and willed herself on to a sea of black velvet. She was floating . . . her feet slipped into this black nothingness, then her knees and her thighs, now her shoulders. She thought she remembered someone saying — or did she read it somewhere? — the brain was always the last to fall asleep. She couldn't remember because hers wasn't functioning properly, trying to think was like trying to drink through gauze. Thoughts blurred, misted, turned into dreams.

She woke, it couldn't have been very long afterwards, in a panic of perspiration. Something had awakened her. A noise. She identified the noise. It was rain, plain heaven-sent rain beating an urgent tattoo on the window.

The breath of relief was still captive in her throat when she heard something else. A mouse-scrape, followed by the lightest of footfalls somewhere near the door. This side of the door, or the other? This side. Because now, although she couldn't hear anything, she could sense a presence. It was harrowing to know that someone was there and not know who it was. Cautiously she raised herself into a sitting position and groped for the torch she kept by the bed. Her fingers grasped its coldness and pointed it in what she thought was the right direction.

"Who's there?" she said, her finger depressing the switch.

"Me," said a voice and Jennifer's startled face sprang into the beam of light. "Are you asleep?"

"What does it look like," said Sharon flicking off the torch and switching on the bedlight, which was less brilliant than the overhead light and gave out a pool of soft pink into which Jennifer stepped.

"Sometimes when people just wake up they are more asleep than awake," she said explaining herself. "Did I wake you?"

"No, I don't think so, Jennifer. The rain did."

"It woke me, too. It sounds less fierce in here." She giggled nervously. "Perhaps that's because there's two of us and there was only one of me."

"I know exactly what you mean." Sharon patted the bed. "Come and sit down."

"This is cosy," said Jennifer. "I even like the sound of the rain in here. It's not violent, but more of a companionable chatter."

"I know."

"We've been learning about rain at school. About some places getting too much and others not enough. Scientists have made rain. They've done it by seeding clouds with solid carbon dioxide crystals. They drop them into the clouds by aeroplane or by sending them up in rockets. Of course they don't know yet if artificial rainmaking will ever be possible on a large scale."

"Fascinating," said Sharon.

Jennifer, after sending her a speculative side-ways look, continued:

"Now in some parts of the world, within about ten degrees of the equator, it rains nearly every day and they have forests. The air is hot and damp, humid I believe it's called, and the vegetation gallops."

"All right," said Sharon. "You've made your point. You've listened attentively to teacher and you've learned

247

your lessons well. Now, why don't you tell me what's really bothering you. Is it going to the dentist's?"

"Yes and no."

"Not scared?"

"No," she scoffed, perhaps a shade too vehemently, but Sharon let that pass and said: "What then?"

"We've been learning all about teeth at school. Did you know that the most common cause for toothache is decay?"

"Oh yes, I definitely know that."

"The crown, that's the part of the tooth that's visible, is covered with a hard enamel surface. If the enamel is chipped, I should imagine the tooth will soon decay."

It was like going through a long tunnel, you think it's never going to end and then you sight the tiniest speck of light.

"What can chip a tooth?" said Sharon picking up her cue.

"Biting on something hard."

"How hard?"

"Would a diamond be hard enough?"

"I should say it would. And if you say you've learned all about diamonds at school, I'll crown you."

Jennifer replied with dignity: "I wasn't going to. We haven't done diamonds." Suddenly her dimple pressed deep and she added saucily: "I do know a diamond is a mineral, and like coal, a form of carbon."

"You horrible child," said Sharon, repressing the urge to giggle. "A diamond is beautiful and glittery and woman's most coveted possession. Stop de-glamourising it."

"Yes'm," said Jennifer pretending to look subdued and positively writhing with laughter. "Just going. Sweet dreams."

"Some hope of that. I doubt if I shall get back to sleep now."

Jennifer met her accusative gaze unblinkingly, thrust her hand into the pocket of her sea-green quilted dressing gown, and pulled out several folded sheets of paper. "In that case," — the laughter melted away from her mouth, leaving it without a quirk and adult-serious — "perhaps you'd like something to read." Then she floated to the door, as dainty as a mermaid and as ephemeral as the night that was breaking into day.

The rain steadied into a soft pitter-patter. Soon it ceased altogether, but Sharon didn't notice. She was too engrossed in the hastily thrust sheets of paper which appeared to have been torn from a school exercise book. She hadn't covered much of Jennifer's neat italic script before she realised it was a promising, if highly imaginative, literary effort. A paragraph more and she found herself harbouring the uneasy thought that this could well be the piece of fiction that had landed Jennifer in trouble. Yet how dare she say this was fact; it was the most blatant fiction ever.

It was a tale of smuggling and intrigue and a gift box of sugared almonds. Her pen made the latter sound very sweet temptation. The box was a gift from an overseas colleague, visited by a representative of her uncle's firm. She didn't know she had stumbled on smuggler's spoils until she bit into one of the sweets and broke her tooth on a diamond.

Oh no, Jennifer! was Sharon's instantaneous reaction. You can't get away with that. And yet she had chipped a tooth on some hard substance and Shari had rushed to town in an insanity of haste.

But diamond smuggling! Once again she turned her head away, put the thought behind her. It wouldn't rest, it tickled the space between her shoulder blades. She had to bring it back and look at it again.

It would be a good way of smuggling diamonds into the country, if one had that intent in mind. Overseas representatives carried samples and brought token gifts back, and who would think of looking at something as innocent as a box of sugared almonds.

251

Really! She was getting as fanciful as Jennifer. But the argumentative seed sounded less solid, a small insubstantial something that could blow away. And the tickle between her shoulder blades felt angry enough to scratch.

Jennifer was sitting up in bed, obviously waiting to be sought out, her eyes round and expectant and frightened.

"You don't believe it?"

"I don't want to believe it."

"Does that mean you do?"

"I don't know. But I'm with you every step of the way."

The something that had died came to life in the child's eye, and her shoulders lost their soldier-stiffness. She said:

"Sorry for lumbering you."

"That's all right." It seemed to need more. Sharon added: "Thank you for trusting me." Jennifer's eyes fidgeted guiltily to her hands.

"I didn't," she said with childish candour. "I took a cal . . . a cal . . . "

"A calculated risk?"

252

"Yes, that's it, a calculated risk." She added anxiously: "Please don't be offended. I like you immensely, but I suppose even crooks have likeable sides. I do hope you aren't a crook and I haven't made a terrible mistake. I had to tell someone."

"I'm glad you chose me. I feel honoured. Even if I am a calculated risk."

"Don't laugh at me," said Jennifer. "It's beastly not knowing who's who. Not a bit like on television, there you can always tell the baddies. The men look mean and the women are beautiful. Not that — Oh!"

"It's all right, sweetie. You've just got your own back. Honestly I'm not one of them."

One of them. One of whom? Just who were they? Jennifer had a point. Not knowing was a special sort of agony. She sent her a swift look, swallowing on the unworthy thought that she'd rather not have been involved. If only Jennifer's teacher had taken notice, she

253

had been the first choice, but she hadn't been perplexed enough to want to touch below the surface.

"All right, Jennifer. Let's discuss it. A bit of honest to goodness literary criticism might reveal some interesting facts. You see, love, you haven't given enough detail. If you are going to be a writer you must remember to write down all the things the reader will want to know. Start by telling me how you came by the box of sweets. Did someone give it to you?"

"No, I found it. Oh, it's all right," she said interpreting Sharon's look. "Not *that* kind of find. It was a game we played. Whenever Uncle Valentine went on one of his trips abroad, he used to bring me a present back. He never gave it to me, instead he hid it for me to find. It was such fun. Once I found a doll perched on the window pelmet. Another time a manicure set in the sewing box."

"Where did you find the box of sweets?"

"In the top drawer of the bureau. That was odd. It was kept for special papers. Uncle Valentine would never have put my present there."

"M'm," said Sharon reflectively. "When you bit into the sweet and broke your tooth, did you know you'd bit on a diamond?"

"No, I thought it was a stone. Mummy said it was a diamond. She sealed the box again and put it back in the bureau drawer, and she told me not to tell anyone. She said she'd think what to do. Only . . . there wasn't time. She . . . " Her voice dropped to a hush " . . . died."

Sharon bitterly regretted having to pull back the memory curtain and expose the child's wrung grief. And yet if she could air it more often, let the tears come, the something screwed up and hurt inside might find release. For all their innocence and lack of worldly wisdom babies know a thing or two. When anything hurts them they show a wide mouth and yell their sweet heads off. Age bottles and battles. Jennifer seemed so young to be so old.

"Cry if you want to, pet, but don't upset yourself about you know what." Ridiculous, but she didn't want to put a name to it. Diamond smuggling sounded too absurd. "Try to forget, if you can."

"Will you forget it?"

"I don't see how I can. But I must have time to think before I do anything. Don't worry, I'll sort something out," she said feigning a confidence she didn't feel.

"When you do, will you tell me?"

"You will be the first to know. I promise."

★ ★ ★

Diamonds, best friend or worst enemy? They didn't seem to be bringing her much luck. She was thinking abysmally of the earrings she'd lost when it came to her that if Valentine did have an illicit trade going, the loss of two small stones wouldn't upset him as much as if he'd bought them from a top-line jeweller. That would also explain his lack of insurance.

What ought she to do? What? Phone Tony?

Jennifer said she'd found the box of sugared almonds in the top drawer of the bureau. Odd that that should stick in her mind. Odd. That was the expression Jennifer had used. Her actual words were, 'That was odd. Uncle Valentine would never have put my present there.'

Memory is a funny thing. Once rolling, there's no stopping it.

'Tony Martindale. Recently back from the Continent, a powerful export order heavier.' Someone had said that the day she was sent round to Martindale's as a temporary secretary.

Uncle Valentine would never have put my present there ... Recently back from the Continent ... Uncle Valentine would never ...

Valentine hadn't. At the time he

was still recovering from his operation. Tony had deputised for him. Tony? She seemed to be testing the name on her tongue.

Oh, Tony! Not you.

14

SHE knew that if she didn't carefully guard against it she was in for a heavy dose of emotionalism. She didn't want Tony to be the diamond smuggler. He wasn't perfect. She knew that. But his imperfections, his cynicism, his intolerance, his impatience, were part of him. In accepting him, she accepted them, just as she did his dancing eyes and quick mirth and quicker tenderness. It wasn't any one side of him that tricked a way into her heart but the exciting whole of him, and it wasn't trickery but free admittance. If he was a whit less of anything it would show in his face, take away a character line here, a frown/laugh line there. He wouldn't be Tony any more.

She didn't want him to be a diamond smuggler. That also made him not Tony any more.

She musn't do anything in a hurry. She must be wary of, besides emotionalism, that impetuous streak in her that hurled her headlong at situations. She pressed her fingers up to her temple. Under one she felt the throbbing nerve, a pulse that fluttered like a tiny hurt bird. Hurt, disillusioned, caught up in the welter of the very emotion she was trying to stave off.

Perhaps it's something you can't protect against, there isn't anything marketed to combat a woman's femininity. Perhaps it has to take its course.

He hadn't lied to her. He didn't wholly tell the truth. But he didn't lie. She clung to that, it was like salve on a wound. After a while she felt calmer and her thoughts began to radiate, fan out into little points.

Point One: Shari had tried to contact Tony. What if she had? What if she'd phoned his flat and managed to get hold of him. 'Look, I know about you. I know you've got a nice little smuggling racket going.'

Point Two: Her mind blanked out at point two and jumped defensively to:

Point Three: Tony wasn't a murderer. Even in fear of discovery he wouldn't stoop to murder. Hey. Shari's death was an accident, remember. You *should* remember. Icy roads. Hit and run they said. Who mentioned murder? Scrub out points two and three.

Point Four: Jennifer's near-escape on the third bend was just a near-scrape and there was no connection between that and Patricia Mason's disappearance. Patricia Mason had gone off on her own. Nobody had kidnapped her thinking she was Jennifer.

Anyway, Tony knew Jennifer. He couldn't make that mistake. But he might not be in this alone. It might not be a case of bringing in the odd diamond, but a highly successful, well organised ring. If he'd reported all that Shari told him, assuming she did manage to contact him, to someone else, mightn't that someone have — ?

No, Tony wouldn't let them. Not for
. . . How ludicrous, but the expression
that sprang to mind was — not for
diamonds. Who knew what a man
would do — for diamonds.

Point Five — unhappy point five:
She didn't know Tony. She hadn't
known him long enough. Oh, she knew
the gay companion, the exciting lover
— she closed her eyes and his face
leaped before her; his eyes were no
longer allied to a smile and looked
reproachful. Go away. She wouldn't
be put off. She would own to it. She
didn't know the man.

Valentine — she'd realised at once
that she must tell Valentine — listened
to her attentively, exactly as she knew
he would. Even so, when she'd told
everything, her expression was one of
tense hostility, daring him to laugh.
Had he laughed he would have been her
worst enemy, because at that moment
all she had to cling to was her dignity.
And yet, if only he had laughed! Called
her an absurd child with her fairy-tale

notions and made ridicule of her idea of plots and diamonds and young girls in dire danger. She would have given everything, even her precious dignity, for his eyes to acquit Tony and make this horrible thing out to be her own and Jennifer's lively imagination.

He didn't laugh. She thought his left eye twitched and related this to her defensive look, but his face remained grave, just a little rueful. With baffling directness he said: "We Martindales are a disgraceful lot."

"You?"

"Don't misunderstand," he was quick to follow up. "I'm not admitting guilt. What I meant was, this sort of thing is usually in the blood." His eyes shot to her's, interrogatively. "Did you ever suspect me?"

"Yes." Her naïve honesty lifted his eyebrows. "I thought, well those earrings you lent me, I thought when you didn't create a fuss it must be because you didn't set a high value on diamonds. Easy come, easy go."

"I see." And now no mistake about it, his left eye did twitch, but he suppressed his amusement sufficiently to say: "Nothing else for it, I shall have to confess. I stole back the earrings."

"But why? They were yours, anyway. I made it plain I didn't want them."

He winced delicately. "Too crushingly plain."

"I'm sorry."

"So I thought," — now he looked endearingly sheepish — "if I couldn't gain your love by fair means, I'd get your affection by foul ones. I wanted you to admire my generous nature. I wanted you to like me. I like being liked."

"Most people do. I do like you. But it was a stupid trick to play. I hated the thought of being indebted to you."

"Now the tables are turned. Because it is I who am indebted to you for your generous forgiveness. You have forgiven me?"

"Of course." There was something soothingly compelling, almost mesmeric

264

in the penetration of his steady eyes. His fingers circled her wrist in a clasp that seemed very sure of itself but which, strangely, did not displace her serenity. There was an odd expression on his face which she did not understand, but apart from that she felt more at ease with him than ever before. That was because he had stopped sparring with her in deadly earnest. The game was over. The mastery that had in turn repelled and held her spellbound, attracting her and drawing her irresistibly to him as a man, had gone. Yet she knew at that moment that he wanted her more than ever.

She felt nothing but admiration for the strength of his self-suppression; his performance was as flawless as his chivalry. He was superb.

Her spine eased from rigidity and her wrist wriggled out of his grasp, to be replaced by a warm curl of fingers. "I'm sorry it couldn't be you." Her faintly regretful tone gave a confused impression of contrition and squashed ardour, as if it wasn't a question of couldn't be, but might have been if. He didn't find the if difficult to guess at.

"It's Tony, isn't it?"

Her: "Yes," was barely audible. It incited from him a droll:

"Even though he's been a naughty boy. Does that bother you?"

"Yes."

For a moment he looked thoughtful and again his face wore the odd expression she didn't understand. "Now that you've told me your suspicions, will that be the end of it?"

"No."

"What will you do?"

"Tell Tony, of course." If she sounded surprised it was because she hadn't done so already.

His eyes narrowed. "My dear, that would be most unwise. One does not warn an adversary of one's action."

"There isn't any action, just a warning." Her voice rose excitedly. "I don't really believe he'd let anyone harm Jennifer. If he is part of a ring, and if he does suspect foul play, he'll be the one to take action. I know he'll go straight round to the authorities with a confession and a demand for police protection for Jennifer. Although," — thoughtfully — "I suppose once it is common knowledge, she won't need protecting. Don't you see, she's only vulnerable while she has a secret to tell."

"Yes I do see. I see how vulnerable she is, how vulnerable you both are. I beg you to reconsider. It's madness to tell Tony."

"No, no, *no*! You're wrong. This is the madness, this whispering behind his back. If there is a plot to silence Jennifer, I'm certain he doesn't know about it. He couldn't. If I'd reasoned things out properly in the first place I'd have gone straight to him."

"I see that your mind is made up." His mouth turned down and the little boy in him, which had been squashed until then, came rushing to the forefront. "I've lost you Sharon." It was almost a whine, as if, although he'd conceded victory, he suddenly couldn't believe it. His head went from side to side, and his tone was full of hurt reproach. "Where have I gone wrong? Why are you doing this to me?"

She puzzled: "But I'm not doing anything to you. Oh! I see what you mean. You're thinking of a possible scandal and that the business might be affected. I suppose even a breath of gossip would be injurious. Yes, from that point of view, you might suffer. I'm sorry, Valentine, but I can't just forget about it."

"Can't you? No, I see you can't." He gave an expressive shrug and, to her intense relief, straightened his back. Dignity maintained, he enquired: "When will you tell Tony?"

"This afternoon. After taking Jennifer to the dentist's."

"After — ?" His hands made a butterfly gesture, the slightest flutter, then he said: "Ah, yes! The dentist." He was silent for a moment; his thoughts were deep but not troublesome because a quick smile arrested his mouth.

"The appointment is for four-thirty. I haven't given you the address yet, have I?"

15

"WHY am I going to a new dentist? Why aren't I going to Mr. Johnson's, the same as I always do?" demanded Jennifer fretfully.

"I don't know," said Sharon, kindness edging into her voice as she looked compassionately at the suffering face. The agony of expectation! "I didn't make the appointment. Perhaps Mr. Johnson is ill."

"Mr. Johnson is never ill," she scoffed, her child's eyes too piercingly direct, so that for some unfathomable reason Sharon found herself looking away.

"Then perhaps he's gone on holiday. I suppose the poor man is allowed a holiday. Or it might be that he couldn't fit you in at short notice and rather than wait your uncle made an appointment

270

elsewhere. Now stop being difficult. There's enough to contend with with that other matter."

"That," said Jennifer sliding her a look of intense satisfaction, "has been taken care of."

"Oh? How, may I ask?"

"The telling of it was so easy, that I decided to do it again. I phoned Uncle Tony, not ten minutes ago, and told him everything."

"Everything?" Even though that was what she intended doing, she couldn't stop her voice lilting in surprise. Their eyes were drawn together as though magnetised and something hitherto unadmitted passed from one to the other, an understanding, subtle, yet as distinct as a message, an awareness of what the other was thinking.

"Yes," said Jennifer putting it into words. "It was beastly. It wasn't so much an admission of something I knew, but an accusation. After all, he smuggled the diamond, or diamonds, in. It's pretty ropy accusing your uncle of something like that."

"Yes I can imagine. Did he admit to hoodwinking the customs," Sharon phrased delicately.

Jennifer shot her a crushing look. "Of course. In view of the circumstances he could hardly deny it. He said 'Blow me!' and started laughing."

"What else did he say?"

"He said for me not to worry, and to tell you not to worry, and to consider him in charge." Her voice drifted on an almost airy note, then dived into steel to challenge: "He couldn't understand why I have to go to this new dentist, either."

"We're here," announced Sharon, much relieved. Jennifer had such a convincing way with her that as she looked at the tall building her own thoughts were inclined to flight. Yet it only looked awesome because it was old, just a bit derelict. Once it had been a grand house, the home of gentry, but it had long since been divided into offices and such. She was familiar with the lay-out because she had used the hairdresser's on the second floor. And one unforgettable day, while in the employ of the typewriting agency, she had worked in the top floor office. At the time it had belonged to an accountant but was now empty. Most of the occupants had moved to new premises as the site was required for a fine new road and the building was due for demolition. Nobody had bothered to scrub the steps or clean the windows. The row of dingy brass name-plates was a forlorn reminder of better days. She thought the dentist must be the last to go.

Was it then she began to have misgivings or later, midway between the second and third floor. Her fingertips cringed away from the dusty handrail, yet it was Jennifer who voiced her thoughts.

"It's spooky," she said in distaste.

"Exactly my own sentiments," agreed Sharon. "Let's get out."

But at that moment the street door

slammed shut and footsteps sounded in the hall below.

They exchanged looks. Jennifer's look asked a question. It said: 'They will get me this time, won't they?' It also accused: 'We've walked into a trap, haven't we?' Sharon's look replied: 'Now we can't be sure of that. We don't know that whoever has just come in is after us.'

Instinct kept them quiet. Instinct and fear.

There is no greater fear than fear of the unknown. The illness that hasn't been diagnosed, the pain that hasn't been experienced, the enemy without a face. Imagination fills in the voids, spells out the dreaded word to name the unspeakable illness, gives the enemy a pair of eyes and a nose and a mouth.

It doesn't have to be Tony. It doesn't *have* to be.

She put her mouth close to Jennifer's ear. "Jennifer," she said softly, "did Tony say he'd brought the diamond in. Try to remember his very words."

"He said it was a fair cop and that he was very sorry I'd found out. Were you hoping he'd deny it?"

"Something like that. Although deep down I knew he couldn't. Valentine was laid up at the time. It had to be Tony."

"Why, Sharon? Why?" The small trembling hand steadied in the grip of the larger, quiet one.

"Poor little one. Has it been a big let-down? I know Tony was a hero to you, a super-being incapable of avarice or whatever prompts man to want a larger slice of the cake than the law permits. Or perhaps it's just the spirit of adventure and who knows what drives man when adventure calls."

"But on the telephone he seemed genuinely sorry. I'm sure he regrets it."

"Possibly," conceded Sharon, adding rashly, "but it's a sad truth that a flung dice cannot be recalled."

"Oh!" Jennifer's hand struggled free and shot to her mouth to capture the gasp. "I must be a prize idiot. I don't know why I didn't think of it before." She was choking on this new thought and her eyes, enlarged and horror-stricken, stared out of a pinched white face. "If Uncle Tony is the smuggler, then he must be the one who wants me . . . wants . . . me . . . out of the way."

Sharon, who had been wondering how long it would take Jennifer to reason that out, worked to dispel the pucker marring her own brow and put a coaxing hand on the child's arm.

"You mustn't think that," she ordered. "I believe in Tony." Under her breath she added 'I believe in Tony until he lets me down.'

"Then," said Jennifer, an uncertain smile clinging to the corners of her mouth, "we have nothing to fear."

I believe in Tony until he lets me down. I'd stake my life —

A voice she hadn't heard for a long time pulled her up short, a memory voice which seemed very real. 'Then you're a fool, Sharon. You're far too trusting.'

'Is that you, Aunt Lucy? I thought you'd gone.'

'Of course I've gone. You've been on your own for a long time now. But that doesn't mean you can dismiss me from your thoughts. Didn't I look after you for ten years? Something of me must have rubbed off on to you. For your sake I hope it has. Girl, if you've one grain of common sense in your entire system, use it now! Think. Think of the child.'

Of course, she could stake her own life, that was hers to do with as she wished, but she couldn't gamble Jennifer's.

"There isn't anything to fear," said Jennifer pressing the point with childish urgency, a hint of defiance showing in the bright spots of pink piercing her otherwise pale cheeks. "Is there?"

"No, Jennifer. I honestly don't believe there is. But sometimes it's better not to take chances. Do you understand what I mean?"

"Yes," said Jennifer dubiously. "Where are you going?"

"Not far, I thought if I took a cautious peep, I might be able to see who's down there."

"Can you?"

"No unfortunately. I can't hear anything, either. Wait a minute, now I can see." Her breath caught in her throat as the pacing figure swung into view. She pressed back, but just one unwary moment too late. Tony had also seen her.

"Sharon!" It was a cry, sharp with anguish and yes — relief. It was the sort of call she yearned to respond to with flying feet and open arms and she didn't know how she managed to refrain from obeying the impulse of her emotions and listen instead to the cold voice of caution. She mustn't shelve the possibility that he might want to harm Jennifer.

"What shall we do?" She didn't know whether it was that tight little voice or the clamorous beat of her heart that drummed her into action.

"Make a run for it," she said decisively.

"Down or up?"

"Up. We can't guarantee that Tony is alone. I might be able to delay him long enough for you to get to the door, but we can't know that he is alone. So, it'd better be out by way of — "

"The fire escape?"

"No. That's too obvious. If he has an accomplice that's the place he'd stand guard."

"Then where? Not the roof? I haven't a head for heights."

"Not the roof, exactly. By an unlucky mishap, which could well turn out to be a blessing in disguise, I know another way out. I once worked for an accountant in the top office and one day, close on home time, I was stupid enough to lock myself in the stock cupboard. Everyone called it the stock cupboard but really it was a tiny room with a trap-door leading up into the loft."

"Is that important?"

"Very. On that occasion someone heard me banging like the clappers and let me out. This joker said if he hadn't come along I could have resorted to the loft, as it runs the entire length of the building, and escaped by someone else's trap-door."

"It sounds tremendous fun," said Jennifer, and she could have kissed her for her attempt at bravado, indeed she did, a light feathery kiss that warmed the child's cheek. Then, clued by an explosion of movement below, the steps began to descend beneath their feet as they climbed, not stopping until they arrived, gasping for breath, at the topmost floor.

There was something chilling in the smell of dust and decay and the general air of desolation, and Sharon couldn't divorce herself from the feeling of being cut off from, more than the world, but from common sense and logic. No good thinking it can't happen. It was happening, and the sheer incredulity of the situation robbed her brain of reasoning power. Yet she must reason, must think. Against her will she was being pushed into an insidious position. She wanted to trust Tony against all odds. She wanted . . . But she mustn't think about her own wants. She must look at this thing from Jennifer's point of view. All that mattered, really, was Jennifer's safety. Her own longing, heavy as it was, weighed lightly when balanced with this sobering thought, and although it tortured her to do so she was able to reject the cry of her heart and consider only her responsibility. Past events had made Jennifer her responsibility. Nothing would ever scrub the day of Shari's death from her mind. She was utterly committed.

As she adjusted, the threads of thought wove more closely together. Jennifer had leaked their whereabouts to Tony, and he had wasted no time in pursuing them here.

He was still calling to them. His voice rose from the giant well round which the staircase curved, three steps nearer to every heartbeat. Her mouth felt as if it was on fire, as if the column of her throat held a million burning tears of frustration, of wondering if Tony really was —

But that was a retrograde thought, a denied luxury, a hope insistent and pressing. Oh my darling, by some miracle of chance don't be involved.

Tony was still screaming at them to stay put. Panic clumsy, her fingers tormented the stock-room doorknob, but it refused to yield. Momentarily she closed her eyes, fighting back a feeling of weakness born of despair. It was like getting to the Gates of Heaven and being refused entry. Dear God . . . please.

She knew, with bitter insight, the door wasn't locked, but that the knob was stiff with disuse and that if she could only be granted the gift of time . . . time enough for the trembling to leave her fingers so that she could properly manipulate the round brass object that spilled out of her shaking grasp.

Jennifer whispered: "Sharon!" The call was soft, yet imperious. A command.

"Yes?"

Jennifer's "Listen," was superfluous because the child's cocked ear and intensity of listening made Sharon listen also. Listen to a snapping silence which was so absolute it grated, and magnified the slight noise of her own and Jennifer's breathing. She looked down at Jennifer's face and marvelled at her composure, until a hand popped into hers, a hand that jerked convulsively and betrayed the inner turmoil.

"Why's he stopped coming?"

Sharon unclenched her teeth to say: "I don't know." The quietly spoken admission rang like a haunting echo in her ear and she seized on the one implausible, but nevertheless sweetly delicious thought, because the tight hand in hers was really wringing her heart and she had to give some reassurance.

"Perhaps he's switched interest."

Jennifer moved just sufficiently to chance a glance down.

"Oh yes, so he has."

"He has?" gulped Sharon, blinking back her amazement. "Let me see."

In the hall below, stood two men. From her bird's eye view, Sharon found it difficult to tell whether she'd seen either of them before. She didn't think so. One was slight in stature and build. His friend was tall, with a bulldog neck and powerful muscles straining a window-pane check, blue and grey sports jacket.

No one spoke. No one moved. It was uncanny. Then Tony stirred into action. He began to walk down the stairs. As bulldog neck looked up, Sharon shrank back into the shadows. She crossed her mouth with her index finger, warning Jennifer to remain silent. Tony had joined the two men. They were engaged in conversation. Although intermittent words floated up, Sharon was too far away to get the drift of what was being said, but reading the gesticulations she thought an argument was in progress. The pantomime of motions indicated that Tony was endeavouring to manoeuvre the two men towards the door. He wanted to be rid of them. They weren't, therefore, with him, as she had first suspected. Or, if they were all in this together, he'd had a change of heart, because he was intent on concealing her own and Jennifer's whereabouts. In which case her instinct to keep silent was right. On the other hand, the two men could well be two strangers who, for reasons of their own, had blundered in. If this supposition was right it would be advantageous to open her mouth and loudly declare her presence.

The smell of dust and mouldering plaster was beginning to make her feel sick. It tickled her nose and smarted her eyes. A large black spider crawled out of a crack and —

Jennifer's scream split the silence. The weasel man, bulldog neck and Tony, all looked up. There was an exodus of movement towards the stairs, despite Tony — bless him he was on their side! — who was doing his damnedest to impede the progress of the other two.

"Sharon! Jennifer! Run for it," he shouted.

This time the door opened so smoothly that she gasped, and they were in the stock-room. Devoid of stock it looked larger than she remembered but, mercifully, not as high. The only piece of furniture the room boasted was a filing cabinet. As they dragged it under the trap door, Jennifer said: "I'm sorry for screaming and attracting attention, but it was the spider."

"It's done," said Sharon. "Forget it. Concentrate on getting out."

"Uncle Tony *is* on our side, *isn't* he?"

"Yes Jennifer." The situation did not permit much comfort and for a moment they stopped to hug one another and revel in that thought. Sharon's voice was thick with relief. "Yes Jennifer, he *is*."

"Can he hold them, do you think?"

"I don't know." I daren't think. "Are you blessed with the agility of a monkey? You'll need to be to climb this beastly thing. I'll give you a hoist up, then I'll join you on your perch and we'll both have a go at the trap-door. Agreed?"

"Agreed."

The filing cabinet was easy, the prising away of the trap-door only marginally less so. Was it an omen? Was luck going to be on their side? If only she could shut her ears to the discord of sounds issuing from somewhere below, but not as far below as at first. The fact that nobody had burst in on them proved that Tony was managing to combat both men. But how long would he be able to keep that up? Concern for him flooded her mind.

"He will be all right, won't he?" beseeched Jennifer gruffly.

"Of course," she responded and although she had to tighten her eyes she managed to make her voice sound crisp and convincing.

"Come on, let's have you up."

The flaking ceiling was a dingy grey-white. Jennifer stared hard at the uninviting square of black which had, until recently, been covered by the trap-door, and through which Sharon was proposing to push her. There were bound to be creepy-crawlies.

"Must I go first?" There was a fretful quibble in her voice.

"Of course you must. Be practical," reasoned Sharon. "You're shorter than I am. You can't possibly manage without a leg-up. Are you ready?"

"Yes," said Jennifer meekly. It occurred to her that she was acquitting herself rather badly. In the stories she made up, her heroines were always level-headed, sensible and brave. They wouldn't be frightened of a few creepy-crawlies and mice and —

"Ugh!" she exclaimed in disgust. "Do you suppose there will be rats?"

"Honey," replied Sharon, anchoring her patience with some difficulty, "the two rats pursuing us are more dangerous than any we are likely to come across in the loft." Jennifer allowed herself to be pitched into the darkness without further utterance.

Now it was Sharon's turn. She wondered, grimly, how she was going to manage without a leg-up. For the first time in her life she regretted not having the muscles of a young and healthy P. E. instructor. As she looked up at the black hole she wondered if she was being optimistic or just plain stupid. Only an expert athlete would attempt it without the aid of a step-ladder. Then she caught a glimpse of Jennifer's frightened white face and without another thought she stretched up and firmly gripped the side of the opening.

Slowly, with tremendous effort she began to hoist herself up. Up she went, steadily, slowly, the pull on her arms was terrific and the strain showed in her face. Up, up, from shoulder to elbow her arms were shot with pain and her clutching fingers felt numb. As her head drew level with her hands she felt drained of strength, as if she had nothing left to give and yet, having put in so much effort, she couldn't allow herself to fail. From somewhere she drew an untapped reserve of strength, gambling everything in one last teeth-gritting surge. The space between the filing cabinet and her uselessly dangling legs, widened. She was head and shoulders home, but the effort was making her feel weak and dizzy.

"Please," implored Jennifer's voice, which seemed to come to her through a maze of swaying blackness. *Please*, you must not give in. Not now."

The tender agony, the stricken disbelief in the child's tone revitalised her into further effort. Now she was waist high; a few tense exhilarating seconds later she was able to lever herself the rest of the way until she was able to collapse on the dusty boards. She was unaware of dragging her legs up and in; all she was conscious of was lying flat on her face, Jennifer's exultant voice ringing in her ear:

"You made it. For one terrifying moment I thought you weren't going to, but you made it!"

"I did, didn't I," she said as soon as she had sufficient breath.

But their joy was short lived, far too soon it was mingled with a less acceptable sound: the crude splintering of wood as a human battering-ram was thrust at the stock-room door. They scampered round into viewing position in time to see three bodies, still locked in fight, fall into the room.

With a minimum of movement the weasel man detached himself and began to mount the filing cabinet. If Tony saw him he couldn't do anything about it.

Bulldog neck was more than a match for him and he was having a hard task holding his own.

"Jennifer," whispered Sharon urgently. "You must be terribly brave and go ahead."

"It's dark. I shall get lost."

"No you won't. There's some pipes here. Follow them. As far as I can tell they run the length of the loft."

"What are you going to do?"

"Delay our friend, if I can. We badly need a start. Off you go."

Jennifer looked bleak, but went.

Sharon lifted the trap-door. She waited until the weasel man had secured a hand-hold, then dropped the door smartly into place. Although his shriek of pain and dismay was gratifyingly loud, she knew she had gained only a temporary advantage. She scuttled after Jennifer, and almost fell over her crouching form at what appeared to be a blank wall.

"There's no way through," said Jennifer.

"There has to be," insisted Sharon. They couldn't be balked now. "You stay put. I'll poke around." She returned a few seconds later. "The way is blocked by a water-tank, but there's a gap down the side. We might just be able to squeeze through. Come on." She gave Jennifer's hand a tug. "You first. I might get stuck half way and then we'd both be sunk. If you do get through and I don't, make a run for it."

"Sharon?"

"Yes?"

"Not a very comfortable bolt-hole, is it?"

"Not very. Hurry, love."

"I'm almost there. I'm through . . . now."

"Good," said Sharon. "Be with you in a tick." I hope, she added under her breath.

"I should be wearing my five pounds thinner girdle," she joked. At that moment the intense blackness lifted. She wriggled round to see the weasel man's head rising into view.

There was a moment, half way, when she thought she wasn't going to make it. Reason would dispute that she willed herself slimmer. Adhering strictly to fact, she wriggled through an incredibly narrow space, to grab hold of Jennifer's hand. "Hustle along, now. We're being followed."

"By whom?"

"The weasel man."

"Good," said Jennifer. "I'm glad it's not the big man. He looks strong enough and mean enough to take you in his hands and snap you in two."

Sharon forbore to point out that it would have been their lucky day had bulldog neck chosen to follow them. He could never have got his large frame through that narrow space. Whereas, she knew it could only be a matter of time before his athletically built tiny friend was breathing down their backs.

Uneasiness obliterated the triumph she would have felt at finding the trap-door. She went down on her hands and knees and forced it open. A step-ladder led down into a room identical in size to the stock-room. Then they were clattering down too many steps to contemplate, at an incautiously fast speed. And yet, at risk of breaking their necks, they daren't slow up. And, anyway, the door of freedom lay just ahead, because surely someone must be in the street. A workman. Anybody.

The door rolled open at first touch, as if it had been oiled in readiness or was operated by a magic button and everything was going just too right to swing into reverse and go all wrong.

The wind had the dust of a deserted street on its breath. It lifted her hair and blew it into her eyes. A hand of masculine proportions reached up to take it away and tuck it behind her ear. Her pent-up emotions released in a sigh. Her tongue found just the one word.

"Valentine."

16

"**I**T'S you, isn't it? You sent us here. You — "

"Yes." His eyes were full of pain. "I didn't want to. Look, let Jennifer sit in the car. It will be better for her."

Sharon considered. The weasel man, who had followed them smartly out, stood just one pace behind. She had no alternative. Anyway, it would be less painful for Jennifer to be out of earshot. She nodded to her and watched her climb into the car parked at the curb. It wasn't unoccupied, as she had first thought. Moira sat in the back, looking pensive.

"Why didn't you stay out of it," Valentine scolded. "Everything was going beautifully until you intervened."

"You mean the smuggling?"

"Of course I mean the smuggling," he

replied impatiently. "You don't think liquorice allsorts pay for the standard of living I enjoy."

"I had wondered. Was Tony your partner in crime?"

"No." His mouth was gripped by a boyish grin. "He thought they were return samples from my overseas associates. That was the whole beauty of it. He never suspected. He didn't have to act innocent, he was."

"But you would have had to tell him in time."

"Naturally. Then I would have cut him in. I'm not greedy."

"What if Tony objected? What if he didn't like being taken for a prize idiot?"

"Not prize idiot," said Valentine looking pained again. "Susceptible, maybe. I knew he wouldn't like it. That's why I kept quiet, out of consideration for his feelings."

Her eyebrows went up. She took out four well-worn words, using them for the very last time. "You are so *kind*."

He chose to ignore the sarcasm in her voice and said loftily: "I would have explained everything to him. In time he would have seen it my way. I'm good at talking people round."

"I believe that," said Sharon with feeling.

"You were my biggest failure. A girl without a price. Most girls say 'You give; I take'. I'd have given you anything. There's a certain sweetness about you I shall miss. I'm sorry it's necessary to dispose of you."

"Dispose?" she said tonelessly.

Now his eyebrows went up. "Why else would I direct you to this deserted place."

"Less messy than your own door-step?" she risked.

"Precisely."

His cold-blooded cheek incensed her. "You can't just dispose of people because they know something about you. Smuggling is bad, murder is worse."

He shrugged his shoulders indifferently.

298

"A crime is a crime."

She blinked away her disbelief. "How can you contemplate murder and stay so calm. Unless — ?"

His eyes narrowed. "Yes?"

Strange how things suddenly hit you. Sharon had never seriously believed Jennifer's tale of attempted murder on the third bend. But it was probably true. Although, he hadn't been after Jennifer, but Shari. That try had, of course, failed. So then he'd followed her up to town and waited his opportunity.

"You. It wasn't a hit and run that struck Shari down. It was *you*."

"Oh dear." He looked distressed. "Must you bring that sad business up now. You're deliberately trying to make me unhappy. And it hasn't all been my fault. I didn't ask to be plagued with stubborn, inquisitive females. Why won't you be reasonable," he trailed off fretfully. His eye flicked up the street, as if he was looking for someone. "Why couldn't the pair of you leave me be. I wasn't doing any harm."

Too worried to analyse properly, or even think too far ahead, she concentrated on just one point at a time, before moving sluggishly to the next.

"You can't have another dead body," she said.

"No dear. Too many corpses, accident victims, set people thinking. You'll just disappear."

She paled, but said bravely: "Without reason?"

A bitter-sweet glint of something touched his eye, approval, regret. Sadly he said: "Nobody disappears without reason. In your case it will be the earrings. They proved too big a temptation."

"But I've already reported them lost."

"My dear, you won't be the first thief to report something missing. Anyway, who do you think believed you? It's too improbable a tale. One earring yes. Two? Nobody loses two earrings."

"All right. So you'll have to report the theft to the police. Otherwise it will give rise to speculation."

He said with slight emphasis: "No, I *won't* have to report it to the police. I don't want them ferreting round. Yes, it *will* give rise to speculation." She understood. He didn't have to add: "I've earned myself the reputation of not only appreciating women, but paying for my appreciation. I shan't consider a pair of earrings extortionate."

She said flatly, without hope: "I'm not that sort."

"I know. But will anybody stand up and testify to that?"

No. In truth, nobody. And Mrs Lamb, her ex-landlady, would foster the idea. 'I always knew she was a bad lot. Brass faced with it, too. Came in one day at four a.m. and when I challenged her she said she'd been with a man. Bold hussy. I sent her packing, of course.' Mrs. Lamb would have a field day.

But no one can disappear into thin air. Someone would miss her. Aunt Lucy, when she didn't write. But would she do anything? People tend not to. What if Aunt Lucy chose to say 'Inconsiderate girl! Going off like that. You'd have thought she'd have shown me some consideration for the years I looked after her.'

She recognised how vulnerable she was and for the first time she was truly frightened. But no, no, *no*. What about Tony and Jennifer? They knew. They'd have to be suppressed. Three people couldn't disappear with no questions asked.

Excitedly she said: "Tony?" But it was such a fragile hope which splintered her voice, because even as she spoke she knew he would have it all worked out, clearly, analytically.

He answered literally. "The big man will take care of him." Once again he glanced up the street. This time she saw a flicker of unease. Interpreted: The big man was taking longer to deal with Tony than he'd anticipated. "He has his instructions."

The big man hadn't dealt with Tony

yet, so she could shelve that bitter implication to ask: "Could you explain his disappearance?"

"Disappearance?" His eyebrows rose significantly. "My dear girl. I'm having a heck of a job explaining his presence. People are thinking I'm spineless allowing him to stay. The way he's been carrying on with my wife." She clenched and unclenched her hands, remembering a time when she'd thought that herself.

"He hasn't. We both know that."

"Do we?"

She was already in shreds. He didn't have to add that. She bit her lip.

"Jennifer, then?" He could explain her's and Tony's speedy exit it seemed, but even he couldn't effectively explain Jennifer away. And yet she couldn't stop her voice pitching into desperation, because everything fitted so perfectly, everyone had subconsciously been working towards his end. He wouldn't let Jennifer stop him. He would have worked something out for her.

"Jennifer?" Without surprise she heard

the lilt of perplexity in his voice. "What about her? Naturally I shall continue to look after my late niece's daughter. No problem there." His voice was biscuit crisp.

"You mean . . . " Even though she had conditioned herself to expect a serene and untroubled front 'head' quarters was momentarily thrown off balance. She had to thump her brain into active response. "You mean you'll spare Jennifer? But . . . but aren't you afraid she'll tell?"

He appraised her for a moment, his face set and serious. Then his lips moved up over his white teeth and his eyes narrowed in a web of laughter wrinkles.

"That's the lovely part. She'll tell, all right. She'll shout it from the house tops, but," — his voice collapsed under the strain of that ghoulish laugh — "who will believe her? Just answer me that one. The child is such a born story teller that anything she cares to say will be taken as just another of her weird fabrications."

Fiendish, horrible; she hadn't words to express her thoughts. Her body writhed with an intensity of feeling. At least her's and Tony's fate would be quick. To know and not be able to make anyone believe would be a living hell. Worse than death.

"If she can't communicate, if no one will listen, she won't be able to cope. She'll go mad."

His face underwent a sudden change. His eyes melted with concern.

"My dear, you must be sensitive to my thoughts because that's exactly my own fear. There has never been any insanity that I know of, but I suppose that sort of thing crops up now and again even in the best of families." He sounded deeply sincere, immeasurably distressed. She was glad Jennifer couldn't hear. Her eyes edged into the car. She saw Jennifer's white face and tightly clenched mouth. She felt worse than useless, inadequate, sick.

Valentine moved over to the weasel man and said something to him in an undertone. "We've decided to take a little ride," he told Sharon. "Sit in the front by me. My friend will sit immediately behind you. In case you decide to do anything foolish." When she didn't instantly move he said: "It would be foolish not to get in the car. My friend is a Judo expert."

As Sharon got in the car she looked at Moira, but Moira looked away. Not in shame, there was something defiant in the lift of her chin. A melancholy whispering glanced across Sharon's mind. If there was a way out, it wouldn't be through Moira.

Silence sat with them in the car. Valentine's eyes anxiously roamed the street. Looking for signs of activity from the building she and Jennifer had so trustingly, foolishly, entered and where at this very moment Tony was probably fighting for his existence.

The car sprang to life under restless fingers and moved from the curb.

Sharon wondered where he was taking them. For a little ride, he'd said. Until the big man had dealt with Tony, perhaps?

"Where are we going?"

"Does it matter."

Her eyes flew open. It didn't sound like Valentine at all. His voice was so strange, harsh, breathless, not like him at all. The car, instead of picking up speed, began to buck, not taking kindly to slinking along at less than five miles per hour. She had seen learner drivers get away from traffic lights in this ungainly fashion. But Valentine wasn't a learner driver. He was — ill?

Simultaneously, several things happened. Moira screamed. Valentine slumped over the wheel. The car slewed to the opposite side of the road; the engine stalled and shivered to a halt.

Decisively Sharon got out, walked round the bonnet and opened the rear door for Jennifer to get out. Nobody offered to stop them. The weasel man look stunned. At first Sharon wondered if he'd bumped his head and was just a bit concussed, although they'd been travelling slow enough for the jolt to be a mild one. Then she realised it was the unexpected turn of events that had left him bereft of thought. Perhaps he didn't think; perhaps he just obeyed orders.

Moira got out of her own side and leaped in beside Valentine. She lightly touched his arm and he rolled over on to her lap. Her hand moved to stroke his hair. As her eyes gathered brightness she said:

"I've told him over and over again, you can't plan. Things never go the way you want them to. Something always crops up to spoil them." She was blinking rapidly and a shimmer of tears spangled her lovely deep iris eyes and pointed her lashes with diamonds. "Dear Valentine," she said over and over again. "Dear, dear Valentine."

Sharon didn't move; there didn't seem to be any particular hurry.

And, foolishly perhaps, she wanted to comfort Moira. It didn't seem to matter that she'd been part of a diabolical plot. At that moment she was a wife, any wife, comforting a husband, any husband.

She didn't see the weasel man take off down the street; she didn't see Tony come out of the house. She saw Jennifer's face see Tony coming out of the house. The fierce set of her mouth crumpled and her fingers, which had been tightly clasped in Sharon's, ran away. To curl round his neck and cling like a limpet.

"Room for two?" queried Sharon lightly. "I refuse to wait my turn and the little one's not going to be easily ousted."

"Would you want to oust her?" He said that as if it was a deadly serious question and not a returned flippancy; and he didn't mean now, this moment, but all the moments, all the years.

"No," she said, matching her tone to the gravity of the situation.

"Still want to come?"

"Yes please." Now, this moment, all the moments, all the years. Then she sprinted into that inviting arm with a fervour that outstripped even Jennifer's. "Oh, Tony! Tony, Tony, *Tony*!" His fingers dug appreciatively into her waist, his eyes paid homage. Then, reluctantly he eased her away.

"Must fetch a doctor."

Desire melted into concern as she looked at him. At the inflamed eye disappearing into puffy painfulness, at the cut, swollen mouth.

"Tony! You're hurt."

"Not me," he said expending a testy brevity of words. "Him."

She had momentarily forgotten Valentine.

"Coming?" invited Tony.

"No. I might be able to help here."

"I'm coming," insisted Jennifer.

She watched them plod down the street before turning back to the car. Apart from the fact that the weasel man had gone, the scene was exactly as before. Valentine's head still rested on Moira's lap, and she was still stroking away, crooning and lamenting into his hair.

She looked up as Sharon drew near; her eyes, as devoid of expression as glass, met Sharon's unseeingly. Still Sharon could not apportion blame. In all the pain and tumult there emerged one golden certainty. Moira had done what she had to do for love of a man. Nobody mattered, no sacrifice was too great — for Valentine.

She was conscious now of Sharon's cool scrutiny and a flicker of fire leaped into her answering glance.

"You didn't know him," she said. Her voice was as challenging as a sword, her eyes fierce and accusative. "You couldn't have known him or you wouldn't have hurt him the way you have."

"Me?" said Sharon idiotically, wanting to protest but not having the stamina to grapple with words.

"Yes, *you*. Spiking his plans. Involving

him in all this extra upset and excitement. You knew it was bad for him. You knew. Why couldn't you have been like the others?" she lashed scornfully.

"The others?"

"You didn't think you were any different, did you? He admitted to being deliciously distracted, but it was a phase. It would have passed. It always passed."

"Yes, I'm sure," said Sharon. "Please don't upset yourself."

"I'm not upset." Her voice rose hysterically. "Not the least bit. You couldn't have held him, you know, once the novelty wore off. He only looked at you because he thought you would be useful to him."

"I know. I *do* know."

"He would have come back to me. He would . . . he *would*."

"Of course," reassured Sharon. "Look, Tony's gone for the doctor. He won't be long."

No answer. Just a look of mute

agony. A look that tolled mournfully in Sharon's mind, telling her what she hadn't realised. Valentine was beyond human help, beyond earthly suffering.

Valentine was dead.

17

"IT has all the unreality of a dream," said Sharon. "I can't believe it's happened. Any of it."

It was much later. They were in Tony's flat. Jennifer was upstairs in bed. In a while Sharon would join her. Sidestepping a delicate situation, Tony had booked in at a nearby hotel. He made Jennifer his excuse but anyway, events had temporarily dampened ardour. The arms wrapped round Sharon were a brother's arms.

"Don't think about it," he advised.

"I'm trying not to. But it's almost impossible. I can't get out of my mind what could have happened. We could both be dead, buried in some remote forest or dumped at the bottom of a lake. And Jennifer, bless her, could be imprisoned in a living hell. Nobody believes an imaginative child. Jennifer's most precious gift, which one day I'm certain will impress itself in print, could have been her greatest tragedy. Her teacher didn't believe when she tried to tell her."

"You believed."

"That's because I'm out of the same imaginative mould. And even I didn't act. I blame myself bitterly for — "

"Don't say it."

"I must. For being underhand and secretive and not trusting you."

"Remember, I didn't trust you."

"But I gave you cause. I should have told you — "

He prompted: "Now I'm interested. Told me what?"

She looked at him from under a flicker of eyelash. "That Shari phoned."

"When?"

"That night. *You* know."

In knowing his face whitened. "What are you trying to say?"

"I invited Shari round for a feminine natter. If I hadn't she might — "

His face cleared. "No one is responsible

for life, Sharon. It was an accident."

But was it? Hadn't Valentine admitted — But Valentine was dead. What good could she achieve in raking up the past. And anyway Tony had been hurt enough without having the weight of that on his mind.

She repeated dully: "Yes, it was an accident."

"But you don't think so?" he said perceptively.

She drew on a deep breath. "No. I wasn't going to tell you, I couldn't see the point in hurting you unnecessarily, but I can't have you thinking I'm still hiding something from you. I think, that is I'm pretty certain, Valentine deliberately ran Shari down. But all parties are dead and, without proof, it's better if suspicion died too; if it can be quickly forgotten it will be a better atmosphere for Jennifer."

A thoughtful pause later he said: "I agree."

"About the other business," she began tentatively. "What do you think the authorities will make of it?"

"I don't know. It had to be reported. My uncle wasn't in this alone. And as things stood I was wide open to blackmail. I am guilty of smuggling goods into the country."

"But you didn't know?"

"Daft carrot. Of course I didn't."

"Then that's all right. You'll get a pardon or a discharge or whatever they call it."

His eyebrows went up. "I wish I had your optimism. Just in case the law is less lenient in its outlook I'll get me a good lawyer."

"Get the best, my darling. I don't want to — " Marry a jail bird, she had been going to say. She snapped it off just in time.

"Don't want to what?"

"No. I shan't tell you."

"Why?"

"Because you'll say I'm being rash and impetuous again."

"If you mean what I think you mean, I'd say more than that. I don't mind

317

your driving me to distraction. I can even forgive you for not trusting me. But I do draw the line at — "

"It's your own fault I didn't trust you," she interrupted, "for telling Jennifer you smuggled in the diamonds."

"But I did," he protested.

"Yes, but for our peace of mind you could have told the truth and said you didn't know about them. Is it them or it, I never know?"

"Them. It's been quite a lucrative business, apparently. What a pity I'm so honest!"

"Don't joke," she reproved, her eyes clouding. "I don't ever want to see another diamond again."

"Never?" he said, picking up her left hand and idly playing with her fingers. He teased: "Where was I before you interrupted?"

"Drawing lines."

"M'm?"

"You said you'd forgive me for not trusting you — my heart did all the time, love — but you draw the line at my saying darling will you marry me. Oh! I've said it, haven't I? I'm sorry, I know a man likes to do his own proposing."

"You know?"

"Not that way. You wretch, it's your fault I'm nervous and when I'm nervous my tongue chatters on and on and I talk a load of rubbish and oh! I do love you so."

"That's rubbish?"

"Stop confusing me!"

"Why should I?" he retaliated, "when you've charmed me into a state of turmoil and confusion since the first moment I set eyes on you." He spoke lightly but his eyes were dark and serious.

She leaned forward and carefully kissed the corner of his hurt mouth and automatically her thoughts touched on the events of the day which had left this scar on what should have been their perfect and beautiful moment.

"Don't dwell on it," he said. "The past is dead."

319

An ache gathered in her throat, misted her eyes and fell as tears. His mouth closed on her cheek pretending to swallow them. His thoughtfulness, his patience and sweetness increased her sense of guilt.

"I'm sorry, Tony." It was unforgivable to be with one man and think of another, and yet she couldn't think of Valentine as a man, only a poor misguided little boy. "It's the waste," she said. "He could have been anything. He could have reached the heights."

"Instead of which he chose to be wicked and selfish," said Tony. She needed him to say that. Things clicked into their proper perspective and she stopped romanticising a ghost. And, anyway, why should they be cheated out of their beautiful moment?

"Tony?"

"Here, love. I've been here all the time."

His arms held her as they had been wanting to hold her. Hurt, mental and physical, was forgotten as their mouths came together. Tentatively to begin with, then clinging, as emotion, tender and protective, leaped into passion.

THE END

WITH SOMEBODY ELSE
Theresa Charles

Rosamond sets off for Cornwall with Hugo to meet his family, blissfully unaware of the shocks in store for her.

A SUMMER FOR STRANGERS
Claire Hamilton

Because she had lost her job, her flat and she had no money, Tabitha agreed to pose as Adam's future wife although she believed the scheme to be deceitful and cruel.

VILLA OF SINGING WATER
Angela Petron

The disquieting incidents that occurred at the Vatican and the Colosseum did not trouble Jan at first, but then they became increasingly unpleasant and alarming.

DOCTOR NAPIER'S NURSE
Pauline Ash

When cousins Midge and Derry are entered as probationer nurses on the same day but at different hospitals they agree to exchange identities.

A GIRL LIKE JULIE
Louise Ellis

Caroline absolutely adored Hugh Barrington, but then Julie Crane came into their lives. Julie was the kind of girl who attracts men without even trying.

COUNTRY DOCTOR
Paula Lindsay

When Evan Richmond bought a practice in a remote country village he did not realise that a casual encounter would lead to the loss of his heart.

ENCORE
Helga Moray

Craig and Janet realise that their true happiness lies with each other, but it is only under traumatic circumstances that they can be reunited.

NICOLETTE
Ivy Preston

When Grant Alston came back into her life, Nicolette was faced with a dilemma. Should she follow the path of duty or the path of love?

THE GOLDEN PUMA
Margaret Way

Catherine's time was spent looking after her father's Queensland farm. But what life was there without David, who wasn't interested in her?

HOSPITAL BY THE LAKE
Anne Durham

Nurse Marguerite Ingleby was always ready to become personally involved with her patients, to the despair of Brian Field, the Senior Surgical Registrar, who loved her.

VALLEY OF CONFLICT
David Farrell

Isolated in a hostel in the French Alps, Ann Russell sees her fiancé being seduced by a young girl. Then comes the avalanche that imperils their lives.

NURSE'S CHOICE
Peggy Gaddis

A proposal of marriage from the incredibly handsome and wealthy Reagan was enough to upset any girl — and Brooke Martin was no exception.

A DANGEROUS MAN
Anne Goring

Photographer Polly Burton was on safari in Mombasa when she met enigmatic Leon Hammond. But unpredictability was the name of the game where Leon was concerned.

PRECIOUS INHERITANCE
Joan Moules

Karen's new life working for an authoress took her from Sussex to a foreign airstrip and a kidnapping; to a real life adventure as gripping as any in the books she typed.

VISION OF LOVE
Grace Richmond

When Kathy takes over the rundown country kennels she finds Alec Stinton, a local vet, very helpful. But their friendship arouses bitter jealousy and a tragedy seems inevitable.

CRUSADING NURSE
Jane Converse

It was handsome Dr. Corbett who opened Nurse Susan Leighton's eyes and who set her off on a lonely crusade against some powerful enemies and a shattering struggle against the man she loved.

WILD ENCHANTMENT
Christina Green

Rowan's agreeable new boss had a dream of creating a famous perfume using her precious Silverstar, but Rowan's plans were very different.

DESERT ROMANCE
Irene Ord

Sally agrees to take her sister Pam's place as La Chartreuse the dancer, but she finds out there is more to it than dyeing her hair red and looking like her sister.

HEART OF ICE
Marie Sidney

How was January to know that not only would the warmth of the Swiss people thaw out her frozen heart, but that she too would play her part in helping someone to live again?

LUCKY IN LOVE
Margaret Wood

Companion-secretary to wealthy gambler Laura Duxford, who lived in Monaco, seemed to Melanie a fabulous job. Especially as Melanie had already lost her heart to Laura's son, Julian.

NURSE TO PRINCESS JASMINE
Lilian Woodward

Nick's surgeon brother, Tom, performs an operation on an Arabian princess, and she invites Tom, Nick and his fiancé to Omander, where a web of deceit and intrigue closes about them.

THE WAYWARD HEART
Eileen Barry

Disaster-prone Katherine's nickname was "Kate Calamity", but her boss went too far with an outrageous proposal, which because of her latest disaster, she could not refuse.

FOUR WEEKS IN WINTER
Jane Donnelly

Tessa wasn't looking forward to meeting Paul Mellor again — she had made a fool of herself over him once before. But was Orme Jared's solution to her problem likely to be the right one?

SURGERY BY THE SEA
Sheila Douglas

Medical student Meg hadn't really wanted to go and work with a G.P. on the Welsh coast although the job had its compensations. But Owen Roberts was certainly not one of them!